I0571339

Praise For Harvest Festival

"A brilliantly written and exciting horror novella. Dramatic and terrifying, the ending stayed in my head."
Banshee Irish Horror Blog

"A splendidly horrific adventure that makes me think of the old Quatermass series."
Altered Instinct

"Great example of what long fiction should be, the fluff stripped away, leaving only a rip-roaring story. I discovered this book on the list of Bram Stoker Awards nominees; definitely deserving of the honor."
The Behrg

"What begins as a picture of a typical family scene soon flips into a terrifying fight for survival. A straight through, single sitting read."
Grab This Book

"Reading this in bed at night my heart was pounding and every muscle tense as I willed the family to safety and even when I thought they had a chance, Drinkwater adds more to the terror."
Jera's Jamboree

HARVEST FESTIVAL

KARL DRINKWATER

ORGANIC APOCALYPSE

Harvest Festival

Copyright © Karl Drinkwater 2016 (updated 2023)
Cover design by Karl Drinkwater

Published by Organic Apocalypse
ISBN 978-1-911278-09-2 (E-book)
ISBN 978-1-911278-08-5 (Paperback)
ISBN 978-1-911278-30-6 (Audiobook)

This is a work of fiction. Names, characters, places, and events are a product of the author's imagination or used in a fictitious manner.

Organic Apocalypse Copyright Manifesto

Organic Apocalypse believes culture should be shared. We support far more reuse than copyright law and licensing organisations currently allow. We respect our buyers, reviewers, libraries and educators.

You can copy or quote up to 50% of our publications, for any non-commercial purpose, as long as the awesome source is acknowledged.

You may sell our print books when you've finished with them. Or pass them on to other people and share the love. You buy a copy, you own it.

We don't add DRM to our e-books. Feel free to convert between formats (including scanning, e-formats, braille, audio) and store a backup for your own use.

HARVEST FESTIVAL

CALLUM

Callum climbed down off the tractor and the engine rumbled out to nothing. The peace of the hills replaced low vibration. It was better. He closed his eyes, savoured it. A reward for a day in the mechanical saddle. The silence was complete. He took two deep breaths, was partway into a third huge lungful of cooling air when his breath hitched, and he realised what was amiss. He tilted his head, as if it helped to hear. Silence – but strangely so. Normally there'd be the calls of birds bedding down for the night. Proper silence wasn't usual, unless the birds were spooked by a predator. Still, nothing seemed amiss, and peace is peace.

But then there were shouts from the house, angry raised voices, and a bang. Door slam, probably. He narrowed his eyes in that direction. They were starting early.

It was tempting to put off going in. Maybe spray weedkiller on the plants that sprouted from the courtyard's cracked cement. Perhaps get the toolbox out and look at the springs under the tractor's seat – the vibration was numbing his arse on every pass. The gate at the end of the drive needed raising again, it had dragged through the mud and got stuck. There was always work to keep hands busy round here. And to keep you out –

"Callum!" his wife yelled, opening the side door a crack. "Are you eating with us tonight, or shall I give it to the chickens?"

"Just finishing up," he said, quietly enough that she wouldn't hear properly and would be irritated. But she didn't ask him to repeat himself, and he was left feeling childish. He took one last look at the silent hills. A place a man could get lost. A place a man could find peace. A place where he could be himself, and just *be* a man. But it was time to give it up. One last inhalation of the growing wind that messed with his hair, then he made his way in.

Cerys was shuffling things round in the oven. The hot smells reminded him he hadn't eaten for hours, and his stomach growled like an idling engine. A sweetness to the smell – probably jacket potatoes to accompany whatever steamed in the pans, and baked apples for later. She banged things around in a way that suggested it wasn't only food simmering in here.

He sat at the table to remove his wellies, saw she was about to say something as bits of mud fell to the tiled floor, and cut her off with, "I'll sweep up in a minute."

"See that you do."

"What's eating you today?" He stuffed the thick socks into the boots and flexed his toes, giving them a wriggle to bring feeling back. If she hadn't been in the room he'd have risked sneaking his feet up on the range where warmth could spread from heels upwards. But she bustled, and he made do with wriggling.

"Can you put a box together tomorrow? Nice vegetables, nothing that looks like body parts."

"What for?"

"Our donation for the harvest festival. The new vicar called while you were in the fields. I promised we'd do something."

"The beanpole with the red hair? He's weird."

"He just speaks properly."

"He's not suited to round here."

Cerys faced him. She was squeezing the oven glove in one tight hand. "You don't like anyone religious. It's petty. Just because you don't go to church."

"It's weird to give to others when things are a struggle here. And they're so rude."

"Rude?"

"Give us daily bread. Forgive us our trespasses. Where's the *please*?"

"I don't want to argue."

"Fine by me."

"And *she's* playing up. Said she doesn't want anything to eat."

"She has a name." Mud apparently. Same as his at the moment.

"She's not skipping food again. And not snacking upstairs either. This is the only family time we have. Here, in this room, at this table. Go and fetch her."

"A please would be nice."

"And Michael's not done any of the chores."

"Okay! I'll speak to them both."

"Before I serve?"

"Yes. Just let me sweep up."

"Leave it. I'll do it. You need to wash yourself first too, which takes an age, and I don't want anything burning."

She turned her back on him, fiddling with plates and cutlery. He could see the rear of her neck, the jut of bone at the top of her spine. It seemed wrong. Normally covered with the long hair she used to tie back but had cut off last week without asking his opinion. She looked vulnerable as she stood with her back to him. Too thin. Flesh and bone, only a hint of the curves she had when they met.

Callum knocked on Michael's bedroom door below the sticker that said "Demon-free Zone" but had the word *demon* crossed out and the word *sister* scrawled above it instead. When there was no answer he just went in.

"Oh, hi Dad." Michael was sat at his computer wearing headphones. Sometimes it was like the kid himself was plugged into it. Callum gestured at his ears and the boy slipped them off. "What's up?"

"Food's nearly ready."

"Okay. I'll be finished soon."

"Your mum said you've got chores before eating."

"No, I've done everything."

"Homework?"

"Uh-huh," he said, which seemed to mean yes.

"Bins?"

"Didn't need doing."

Callum glanced round the boy's room. It was surprisingly tidy. Michael had always been a neat child. Horror and astronomy books in a straight line by the bed; the open box he stored some sort of collectable cards in neatly divided into compartments with not a card out of place; even the glow-in-the-dark planets were spaced out on the ceiling in their correct order and relative distances. "Put the chickens to bed?"

That broke the coolness. "Oh. Shit."

"Shit, indeed. And watch your language. Your mother would skin and bake both of us."

"Sorry, Dad. And I did forget the chickens. But can't Maggie do it? She hardly does anything, and I was busy. Like, actually doing *work*, not just putting make-up on and practising snogging in front of a mirror."

"She did it when she was younger. Now you're old enough and the job passes to you. It's called inheritance."

Michael muttered something incomprehensible and turned from Callum. "Right. I'll do it." He clicked on the mouse harder than necessary. Must be some behaviour that ran in the family. Words causing angry jolts in the extremities. Callum was about to move on, mission accomplished, but something stopped him. Maybe there were ways to smooth out the family temper. It was always trickier than just giving a piece of machinery a clang with a wrench, but it could count as maintenance. Oil the machine to pre-empt breakdowns later. He pulled up a chair and sat down next to his son.

"What were you doing that was so important? We've got a moment as long as the hens haven't got out." Callum nodded at the computer screen. "You can show me."

Michael's face lit up, and Callum realised he'd got something right, even if it was only with the least prickly of the house's residents.

"Oh, it's brilliant. An astronomy thing that's on all the groups today – they're picking up a blitzar, and some of the scientists think it's in real time."

"They? Blitz? Real time?"

Michael switched between images and screens of numbers and text, some of which he said were blogs, others chatrooms, others websites. Callum noted that Michael was speaking slower than usual, the patronisation of turning things into parent-speak.

"Okay, there's all these radio bursts in space, right, different types. One that's really rare is a blitzar. It's pretty new in astronomy terms. Like, since I was a kid."

"You're only twelve."

"Exactly. Anyway, this is probably really far away, it's still buzzing round, but it's dead exciting because there's these bursts and we don't even know for sure where they come from, and it's a millisecond pattern. Like, teeny. They say it's a neutron star collapsing, or a solar flare, but I think that's BS. I think it's a signal."

"A signal?"

"Yeah. Not natural. It seems too regular."

"When I was your age I was into astronomy too, but sometimes it's like you're not my son. Have you got an adult's brain in there?" Callum knocked on Michael's head, and was pleased that he still flinched and laughed like a boy. He hadn't lost him yet.

"You told me you learnt the names of the constellations off your dad! That's not really astronomy."

"Oh. I thought it was."

"Don't worry. It was probably still a big deal then. But nowadays we have the Internet."

The boy was gone again, replaced with the patronising young adult that would move into Callum's home in the next year or two. Oh joy.

"Chickens," said Callum as he left.

Music thudded from Maggie's room. Always that thudding with the stuff she liked. Maybe it reminded her of her other favourite sound – doors slamming in temper tantrums.

Again there was no reply to his knock. He even glanced at his fist to check it was still there and tried again. Miraculously, she heard it over the bass.

"What?"

"Can I come in?" It felt ridiculous asking a kid for permission, but it saved trouble later.

"I'm on the phone!"

It wasn't an outright refusal so he opened the door and went into a room which was a total contrast to Michael's. The walls were covered in posters for bands he'd never heard of, though for weeks Maggie had been in the process of taking them down and piling them in the corner with anything else she seemed to think she had outgrown. Her chest of drawers was covered in make-up, much of it left open, along with powder spills and greasy smears. He carefully stepped over clothes, noticing with disgust that some of it was underwear. Better to ignore it, he had enough of a challenge already.

Maggie lay on her bed. Her tights were ripped, though it was style, not accident, and she wore one of her favourite T-shirts, with the bold slogan *You can send me to school, But you can't make me think*. She pulled a face and turned her back on him, continuing to talk into her mobile as if he wasn't there. Industrial noises that wouldn't have seemed out of place in his machine shop came from the tablet computer she'd plugged into some round speakers, backed up by headache-inducing staccato basslines.

"Yeah, well I've got loads," she said into the phone. "But I'm sure yours still go from your ankles to your arse!" A laugh. "You're more than welcome to try some on."

"Maggie, please put the phone down. I need to talk to you."

"Yeah. I'll be out at seven," she told her friend on the phone, ignoring Callum. "Chillax, I know. I keep meeting bloody weirdos."

"Maggie!" he snapped. He hated the kids having mobile phones. There was no way to yank a cable out of the wall when you wanted their attention.

"At least you don't feel like killing yourself every night," she continued.

That was it. He went over to the speakers. Realised they were plugged into the mains and grinned with satisfaction as he pulled the plug and ended the noise.

"What you do that for?" Maggie yelled at him. Then, quieter, into the phone, "Hang on."

"No, hang up."

She glared at him but did what he said for once, saying "Five" into the phone and putting it down before giving him full blaze. "Don't touch my stuff!"

"We bought it for you."

"But it's mine!"

"You should have paid attention to me. Next time I'll drop it in the oil tank."

"You wouldn't!"

Of course he wouldn't. It would get stuck in the filter. But he just stared at her calmly until she said, "You clotpole pleb!"

A twelve-year-old boy he could relate to. A wife who closely resembled someone he fell in love with, he could deal with. But a fifteen-year-old girl was like an alien species. Different values, different looks, and even a different language sometimes.

"Dinner's ready soon."

"I don't care. I'm not hungry."

"And I don't care that you're not hungry. Your mother spent time preparing food for us all. The least we can do is sit and eat it like a family."

"Some family."

"I really don't know what's wrong with you."

"Maybe that's the problem," she said, sparking up to a new level of irritation. "Maybe you like living on a farm in the middle of nowhere. But it would be nice if I lived near my friends. Lived where something was happening. Not have to beg for a lift all the time."

"This is what pays for your clothes. This is what pays for your gadgets."

"So could a proper job if you got one."

That stung. There were times when he itched to throttle her. Tighten things until the septic tank stopped leaking sewage. Or to retaliate with words like she could. But that would just make her worse. And he wouldn't win. She was better at it than he was. The last thing he wanted was more friction here, Maggie storming out angrier than before, Callum failing Cerys' mission and leaving her mad too, and an evening surrounded by seething resentment. He didn't have their sharp words but he did have his innate self-control. Perhaps the fact that it hadn't been passed on to Maggie meant he had more of it for himself.

"Driving lessons," he said, softly enough she'd be forced to listen.

"What about them?"

"Give me a week of peace and quiet; a week where you're nice to your mother, act like an adult; and I'll treat you like one. Take you out in the car. Basics. And if you keep it up I'll pay for some proper lessons after."

Her eyes seemed wider. Like when she used to curl up on his lap as a little girl while he'd tell her fairy stories of strange beasts that roamed the hills and forests of the night.

"Done," she said, and a smile took over, banishing clouds immediately. "I can drive a bit already."

"I don't want to know," Callum said. "Dinner. Pleasant conversation with your mother and brother. Five."

"Dad!" an urgency in Michael's voice that suggested Maggie had done something to him already. So much for bargaining with the devil. Callum wiped his face dry with the towel, pulled the plug from the sink, and put on a clean checked shirt as the dirty water swirled away.

"What's she done?" Callum asked.

But Michael's face didn't look annoyed. It looked excited. His eyes shone, genuine boyish excitement. The good stuff.

"I was putting the chickens to bed and – oh, you have to see this! Mum too!"

"What?"

"Just come!"

Michael didn't wait, pounding down the stairs and jumping the last half dozen with a bang that made Callum think of broken bones. But the boy's voice faded into the kitchen, trying to spread enthusiasm to Cerys.

Good luck with that.

Callum headed down. He'd satisfy the boy. His own curiosity, too. Whatever had fired up Michael wasn't threatening. It couldn't be anything as banal as Beaky starting to lay again. What did that leave?

Cerys and Michael were already outside, the back door ajar. Callum put his wellies back on, noting that they'd been moved and the muck rinsed off in the outhouse boot sink. He followed the wall of the house and workshop to join them at the back, and as he rounded the corner to face west with the whole hillside view in that direction open to him, glowing in the sun's last blaze of orange as it said goodnight, he froze, genuinely surprised.

"See, Dad! Ever seen one o' them before?"

"Can't say I have," Callum replied.

Above the hills, and bordering Carreg Mawr, were discrete cloud formations. But rather than the way sunset clouds normally looked, painted flat and purple across the horizon, these had depth to them, piled up like huge funnels, inverted forms of the mountain. Whether it was that resemblance to something of known size, or just the way they shaded with depth, rounded, impenetrable, deceivingly solid in appearance, they resembled floating behemoths; giant drifting jellyfish of the darkening skies.

"What are they?" Callum didn't take his eyes from them as he asked.

"I *think* they're called lenticular clouds," Michael replied. "Because they're sort of made of layers, smaller round ones at the bottom, bigger at the top, all stacked. Like a pile of lenses."

"Like a spinning top," Cerys added. Her hand found Callum's, almost shyly slipping into place. He squeezed.

"Well, the hills are full of surprises," Callum said, sweating in the strangely humid heat. Then they just watched as the clouds moved slightly, wobbled in the high air winds, their size only seeming to grow in the spreading darkness.

When they returned to the house Callum noted that the chickens weren't making their usual satisfied *prrp prrp prrp* noises as they settled for the night. They just stared at him from the coop's open door.

"Don't forget to lock them up," he told Michael.

MICHAEL

Callum's eyes flicked open. Cerys murmured in her sleep but it wasn't that. He sat up slowly, careful not to disturb her. The furniture shapes were where they should be. It wasn't that, either.

It was too hot and his skin prickled with sweat. Humid, like the prelude to a big electrical storm. The kind of feeling that drove him indoors if he was out on the tractor. He'd get under cover in the barn and watch the sky for the tell-tale dark grey of a thunderhead, or a flash of lightning on a distant peak.

There were no strange noises. Maybe it was just the heat that woke him.

He slid out of bed carefully. Picked up his jeans on the way out of the room, leaving the door ajar so it wouldn't click, and slipped into them on the landing. Sleepy noises from the kids' bedrooms. (Not really kids any more, he corrected himself.)

Down the stairs in his bare feet. He was wide awake, charged. Wouldn't sleep for a while. May as well watch the storm arrive. Elements battling with each other might wear him out. It was so warm he didn't need a top, would welcome any cool breeze on his upper body. He pulled thick socks and wellies on, then unbolted the back door.

It was stifling outside, as close and muggy as any impending storm he'd known. The sky had a faint glow to it that illuminated dense clouds. He followed the house round to take in the view of Carreg Mawr. If it started anywhere, it would begin in that direction. And the heaviness in the air had to break. It was going to be a boomer.

When he reached the chicken cage and looked out across the valleys the sky was different. The wobbling inverted mountains of earlier were gone. Instead the cloud lowered over his farm and the hills beyond, a single layer of murky deep sea, the way fog would settle in lowlands and have depth whilst hiding everything within. A heavy presence flickering with a blue that didn't resemble any lightning he'd ever seen. It was ... unnatural. No breeze. Just a heavy smell of ozone, or something else, which caught in his throat. If it wasn't for the sweat running down his back he would have seriously wondered if he was still asleep. Another ripple of light, deep within the roiling mass, yet bright enough for him to cast a shadow for a second. It had to be a storm, but still ...

There was a clattering sound. Something falling over. In the barn, or the storage shed. Rats were a possibility. Cerys kept saying they should get another cat. He'd put it off because he resented the thought that it was more likely company for her than a practical consideration, and that reminded him of how their relationship had deteriorated, cracking up like the courtyard he never had time to repair.

If rats were around he should make extra sure that food wasn't left out to encourage them. A glance at the chicken coop, which would be a prime attractor with all the seed that got dropped in there. Perhaps he could –

There was a hole in the fencing.

He approached it. The chickens sometimes had the run of the farm, but mostly just this twelve by six yard fenced on the four sides and top. They were safely locked into the shed end of it now, but the fence hadn't been torn earlier. He'd have noticed it when they were stood here watching the clouds. This had happened during the night. He crouched, touched the jagged wire. It didn't look like a fox's entrance, but it was possible.

A smell again. More than something in the sky. Blood. Charred skin or meat. He saw that the hen's night coop wasn't closed after all. The door stood open. Maybe Michael had forgotten to close it, and a fox had got in, taken the chickens. Callum thumped the wire, rattling it, grinding his teeth at the thought of how severely he'd have been beaten if he'd made a mistake like that on Da's farm. But the rattling was more than expected. Loose mesh. He pulled on it, and realised it was a large flap. A cut, right up the chicken wire. This was not a fox. The gash went up to head height. Human head height.

His nearest neighbour was a mile away. No reason for Brinley to do something like this, they'd always got on well. Had to be a stranger.

He glanced round. Nothing apart from the blue flashes. He slipped into the chicken area through the rent in the fence. Crept up to the hens' night nest. The smell was stronger. He made comforting noises. No sounds from inside. He reached in and felt round, then quickly retracted his hand. Sticky with warm, coagulated blood. Pieces of feathers and skin hanging from it. A smell of charred bone.

It was no fox.

He glanced again in the direction where something had fallen and clanged, a new significance to the noise.

From here he could sneak up to the barn. Peep inside. Find out what was going on; whether there was an explanation that made sense, a situation he could resolve. Only a peep, and he could run back to the house. He had to know more. Protecting his family might depend on it. Leaning against the house wall was a rake, used earlier for dealing with the autumn leaves in the back garden. One of the tasks Cerys nagged them about. He was grateful for once as he snatched it up. It wasn't the most intimidating weapon on the farm but he was reassured by the pole of wood, and the metal spikes at the top.

The blue flashes in the sky were irregular, not continuous. He waited until one had finished blooming in the clouds, then dashed to the side of the barn. No flash, no giveaway shadow. He pressed against the rough wall of the building. Edged towards the entrance. There were crackling sounds coming from inside. A smell that could be from the air, but seemed too strong. It resembled the hot metallic smell of welding.

Another clatter. Far in, near the back. Good. Callum peered round the corner. Clear. He crept along the fronting to the open entrance. Darkness within, except for a strange blue flicker. Something electrical at the back. Someone using tools, maybe, though none of his should spark in that way unless it was faulty. Apart from that he could see the usual shadows: rolls of packing plastic; stacked pallets; his heavy machinery in the middle. The movement was beyond that. Another electrical crackle, another flash, and he saw a shadow cast for a brief stuttering second against a side wall. Distorted, maybe by the perspective, but humanoid. It had to be a person. And they were tall. But it wasn't quite right. Too tall. Callum thought for a second of the new vicar, the way he seemed to look down on Callum (literally and figuratively). He'd never trusted religious people, with their strange ceremonies and festivals that didn't make sense. What would the vicar be up to here? Were the chickens his doing?

Sky flashes behind him, crackling blue sparks in front. He moved quickly to one of the massive wheels of the combine harvester. The sparking continued. From here he could see the person's shadow more clearly with every static burst. It was all wrong. Perhaps it wasn't human after all, just a random shadow made up of machinery shapes jutting out and in line with an electrical fault's outburst. Maybe Callum's pounding heart was wrong to be pushing him to the edge of panic. It wouldn't be the first time he'd been made into a fool.

By now he'd reached the driver's cab of the harvester. He moved more confidently to the corner, and had started to look round when there was an awful scraping screech and sudden movement towards him. His legs nearly buckled in fear at the brief glimpse of the thing – just enough for a mish-mash perception that included raw flesh, metallic parts, fused in some nightmare way that he instantly knew wasn't make-up, or trickery – it was real, it was alive, and it shouldn't have been. He was thankful he didn't see it in full detail. And grateful he didn't see it up close.

He sprinted out of the barn. A crash behind him, things over-turned. Don't look back. It was hard to run with the rake, it almost tangled his legs as he ran across the courtyard. Scraping sounds on the cement, a feeling of warmth on the back of his legs, as if it was right on his heels, or emanated vast amounts of heat; either way it kept him running, focussing on the back door, within reach if he didn't fall. He threw the rake behind him, aiming low without looking back, and the scraping and thudding did change in pace, fell behind fractionally; maybe not enough, but now his bare arms pumped away, legs lifting, hoping the wellies wouldn't trip him; he saw the open door, knew he'd been a fool to explore, leaving his family asleep and vulnerable; and then it was over, and he plunged through the back door, slammed it behind him in the darkness of the kitchen, one bolt, two, something heavy smashed into the door; it held, but not for long; the fridge was next to the door so Callum grabbed it and heaved it over onto its side, bottles inside smashing, the fridge falling open, but it was an extra heavy barrier which he was grateful for when another huge thud rattled the bolts. He leaned against the door, hands planted on the wood, pushing, and after another crash it went silent. He tried to clear his mind of the image of machinery and flesh being fused together, fought the twisting in his gut, looked around instead. Nothing else to pile up nearby, and pointless with a fragile window above the sink just a few feet to his right. He backed away, listening for any noise, any scrape, but his heart thumped so hard he couldn't hear movement out there, any moment expecting the glass to break. A blue flash outside the front made him jump, but he realised it was one of the deep cloudbursts, not the sparking of that *thing*.

The chain was on the front entrance. He closed the inner kitchen door silently, backed up to the stairs, heard a creak from behind him, sensed a presence, raised his fist hopelessly at the shape, he'd go down battering; but then it spoke, his name, "Callum, what is it?" with fear in the voice, Cerys huddled in her dressing gown. "I heard the crash in the kitchen, what's going on, is it burglars? The lights aren't working and –"

"Dad?" another voice called from upstairs, Michael.

"Up. Get up the stairs now, get the kids."

"What is it?"

A noise somewhere outside. Like a scraping on brick. Nails pulled out of an old board.

He pushed her ahead of him, no point trying to secure downstairs, it would take too long, he needed to get his family together, get his thoughts together, calm down the racing blood. "It's okay," he said, half to calm Cerys, but half for himself.

Michael was on the landing in slippers and pyjamas, looking like the little boy he used to be. "Dad, I think there's someone outside," he said. "In the shadows when I looked out of my window."

Callum whispered, "We'll be safe in here. Michael – make sure Maggie's awake. Fetch her here."

Michael nodded, went into Maggie's room without knocking, murmured voices from in there.

"It might be worse than that," Callum whispered to Cerys in the moment they had alone, as she gripped his arm tightly. "I went out, and saw something I can't explain. I think it's dangerous. Go into the bedroom, ring the police. Please do it now while I watch the stairs."

And Cerys didn't argue. She let go of him and moved warily into their dark bedroom, despite her obvious fear. And he remembered the strength in her, the time she'd twisted her ankle but insisted on walking home, the way she dealt with the painful birth of the kids, her need to be doing things all the time – he remembered it and was grateful for it.

He looked over the bannister. Stairs down to the hall. Empty. No noises from there. A door opened behind him. Maggie yawning. Michael at her side. "I can't turn it on, Dad."

Callum realised his son held a mobile phone.

"Battery?"

"No. I charged it before."

Cerys joined them. "The phone is dead. Like I tried to tell you, with the lights."

Callum stepped over to the landing switch. Flick. Nothing.

"But there was electricity in the outbuildings ... unless it was from another source."

"Another source?" asked Michael.

They were all keeping their voices low. Maggie picked up on the tension, asked what was happening. Callum left Cerys to say something, to watch the stairs. He crossed the landing and looked out of the window into the backyard area. Apple trees. Piles of leaves. Bushes. A hundred hiding places. No movement. Michael joined him, said "Wow!" when he saw the sky, the way it tumbled low and heavy.

Then it happened, an eye-searing flash different from the others, blue crystal lights shot down out of a cloud, exploded into sapphire spots then faded away just as quickly. Another, nearer, in the back garden. The light seemed to melt into the ground. Michael covered his face and moaned but Callum squinted through the watering eyes, watched the ground, needing to know more, what this new sign meant, what threat it might offer. It wasn't lightning. Too straight; sparkles in it, unlike anything natural. Broken, crystalline. It was more like a beam, coloured torchlight through dust motes and glitter, somehow stretched, drawn. And near where the light had dissolved, there was movement. His eyes were still dazzled, so he couldn't make it out clearly, but something merged with the shadows of the trees.

Callum yanked Michael back, out of the view of the window. Out of sight of anything among the trees.

"That was bright," Michael said, uncovering his eyes. "It wasn't lightning, was it, Dad?"

"No."

"It was pixellated."

It was something worse than pixies, but Callum was torn between telling them how terrified he was, how much danger he suspected they were in; and trying to keep them from panicking. He took a slow breath. Cerys did yoga sometimes and said it helped. He normally rubbished it. Now he'd try anything. He looked at their scared faces and inhaled deeply again.

"I'm sorry to scare you. But I'm going to tell you the truth. I went outside to see the storm, there were noises in the barn. I looked and there was ..." He was talking too fast. Slow down. "There was something there. And I don't think it was human. I didn't imagine this. I wish I did." Cerys put one arm around each of their children's shoulders. They didn't resist. "It chased me. I got in the kitchen, barricaded the door. I think it's still outside.

There's something wrong with the storm. The blue lights, it's electrical, but not lightning. I saw some kind of flashes coming out of the clouds. Into the garden. And I think it's more of them. Things, like in the barn. Like outside the house, now. "

"Were the lights teleports?" Michael asked, seeming to overcome his fear with wide-eyed interest.

"You tell me."

"So they're *aliens*?"

"I don't know that, either."

"Maybe they come in peace?"

Callum thought of the chickens. "I don't think so."

"What are we going to do?" asked Maggie, a vulnerable waver in her voice he hadn't heard since she hit her teens.

"Make sure all the windows are closed, and shut all the curtains. Maybe they won't see us. You three do the upstairs, I'll go down."

"No!" Cerys said sharply. "We stick together!"

"They're outside. It's okay. I'll check quickly." And get a knife, Callum thought. Or even better – go into the cellar where his gun cabinet was bolted to the wall. It would only take a few minutes to take out his shotgun and load it. Maybe the cellar would be a better place for them to hide, since there was only one way in? But then he remembered the feeling of weight to the thing that chased him; its speed and power. They'd be trapped in a dead end. No, just do what he had to do, get back up quickly.

Michael was already pulling the curtains over the landing window, which prompted Maggie to go into one of the bedrooms. Good. Cerys' face was pale. Callum's was probably just as bloodless right now.

With the landing curtains closed it was darker, but enough of the blue light came from outside to see vague outlines. He crept down the stairs, which creaked under his weight. Old houses, old wood. Glanced over the bannister. The hall was as he'd left it. The hulking shape at the edge of his vision was just the coat rack. Sweat trickled down his still-bare chest. The heat was overwhelming. As unnatural as everything else this night.

At the bottom he approached the front door. Good, solid wood. There was time for a glimpse through the peephole, see if anything was moving at the front. If they needed to make a run for the car he'd like to know there was nothing nearby. He had to force himself to breathe; he kept involuntarily holding his breath, ears straining for the slightest sound. He'd just begun to move his eye to the spyhole when the letterbox moved in front of him.

The flap was lifting.

He flung himself to the side, back to the wall, out of the line of sight, heart pounding. He prayed that Cerys and the kids would keep quiet, not call his name to ask if he was all right. The letterbox was now open, and something reached in ... not fingers, surely; too long, and although there was a glisten of raw flesh, there was also a bluish shine of burnished metal, and some wire-like cords which twitched within and around it all. It seemed to pause, as if taking in the air; felt around, looking for a handle (though that would imply understanding), or just to assess the portal's size; then with a jerky spasm it withdrew and the letterbox closed. No noise. It was either silent as it moved away, or it was still on the other side of the wall he leaned against.

He didn't want to move, but couldn't stay there. The longer he waited the more chance that one of his family would call his name and attract attention, or it might try again, or the bastards could get in through a window. What if they could climb? The thought of them getting upstairs while he cowered here spurred him into action. Thankfully the rubber soles of the wellies made no noise as he crossed the hall to the cellar stairs, eyes scanning every doorway then back to the letterbox. Go down, get the gun first. Then check the ground floor if he felt like there was still time.

Noises upstairs, curtains closing, light footsteps, that was fine. Blue light, like cold moonlight, revealing some shapes, leaving others as pools of darkness. Mystery that he could do without. He glanced into the living room. Okay. A clock on the wall. It had glow-in-the-dark hands and numbers. He spared a few seconds to investigate. It wasn't ticking; hands displayed 10.52pm, but it was now the middle of the night sometime. The clock ran off a battery, so the problem wasn't just to do with the mains.

He was opening the cellar door when there was a crash from the kitchen. Not a window – this was more like a glass or a bottle being knocked onto the tiled floor, a noise he'd heard often over the years. He thought of the sauce bottle on the kitchen table in the centre of the room. Yes, the noise had come from nearer the hall he now stood in than the back door.

Something was in the kitchen already.

Forget the gun, the cellar. If the things could move that quietly when they wanted to, and there was one on the other side of the kitchen door he was staring at, then he needed to move his arse *right now*, and get up to his family.

On the balls of his feet; he passed that door, staring, listening, but moving quickly. Definitely a noise in there. Dragging or scraping.

"Callum?" It was Cerys, upstairs. Movement in the kitchen, a reaction to the sound. No point sneaking now, he pounded up the stairs, all three of them there, no point going into a bedroom; think, think; landing window, but that was a drop, into the trees and bushes and shadows where they roamed; thuds from the kitchen; get away from it, higher, he looked up; "What is it, Dad?" asked Maggie, trying to grip his arm, but he shook her off; hatch to the attic, yes. He snatched the hooked rod from next to the plant pot where a lemon geranium sprouted, releasing a hint of citrus, something more hopeful than charred flesh and sparked metal; reached up and hooked the hatch, pulled, with a click and tremendous squeal from hinges *he really should have fucking oiled* the hatch lowered, he could reach up, grip the ladder, unfold it down, aware of movement in the hall and the noises from his family, words, panic, ignore them, ladder down now, "Get up, now!" he snapped, no need for silence as Michael scrambled up there, always quick at climbing, Cerys pushing Maggie next, doing the right thing, and he loved her for that; he heard the stairs creak more than they had for him, creaked with real weight, he was shoving Cerys, hands on her arse and pushing her up ahead of him, not turning to his left where the top of a shadow grew, misshapen but don't look, heavy but ... up the ladder himself, the kids pulling Cerys, enough space for him to just grab the loft hatch and pull his body weight up rather than wait for the ladder to clear. The ladder wasn't meant to be pulled up from inside, not designed for it, but he lay on his stomach and reached down with the hook, grabbed a rung, pulled, hoped it would work, and with protesting hinges it did lift, even as something reached out to grab it, with limbs that weren't arms but were ... no, ignore, he heaved with all his strength and the ladder folded, flew up, closing the hatch with a click. He jammed the hooked rod through the ladder's mechanism, hoping that would block it, stop it from being lowered. Saw Cerys hugging both the kids to her, their faces hidden, all panicking, all sobbing, and he was pleased, relieved, because there were three of them and they were with him.

Something banging on the attic hatch, ripping into it, spiked, tip showing through, but the hatch stayed closed. Crashing from below, no stealth now, destructive sounds and a screeching robotic fury, nails down a blackboard. Callum threw his arms around his family and squeezed them all, huddled in the dark. If not safety, then at least respite.

The attic was half converted. He'd put in skylights, blocked off the water tank, and put a basic floor over the joists. Cerys had nagged him to finish it off with plastering, electric sockets, lights and carpet, so she could have a room of her own. He'd never got round to it. Joked she could be a mad woman just as easily downstairs. She hadn't been amused.

It was bright enough to see, with the blue flashes and residual light from the sloped windows. He glanced round the dustiness and wished he had finished the conversion. Then there could have been all sorts of useful things up here, rather than just water (if they could bring themselves to drink from the immersion tank). But he was always so busy.

He crawled over to the corner where there was an irregular shape. Some offcut bits of wood he'd not tidied away. Most were too small to be useful but one was about two feet long and had weight to it. Better than nothing. He took it and crawled back to his family.

"We should be safe up here," he whispered. "With the ladder up they can't get in. Must be the middle of the night, so it will be day before long. A few hours. If we wait long enough they'll go away." He hoped so, but didn't feel as confident as he tried to sound. "Or help will come."

It had gone quiet. That was more worrying than the furious noises, knowing how stealthy these things could be. Callum lay on his stomach, ear to the floor near the hatch, straining to get the slightest clue as to what they were doing. There was a creak from below, floorboard bending under load perhaps, or just settling.

"Maybe they're retreating," Callum whispered. Some hope, but he wanted to reassure his family. "If they are, then we could –"

He was interrupted by a spike of some sort piercing the floor a few inches from his mouth. It glistened in front of him, then slid down with a scrape.

He'd just sat up, kneeling when another punctured the ground where his head had been. It sizzled with heat, a vapour of smoke from the scorched board flooring, then scraped back. Red light shone up for a second, laser-like in its precision, then another hole was made, near his left knee.

"Back, against the eaves!" he said, gesturing at the lowest bits of roof near the outside walls. "Now!"

They shuffled back. Callum rolled on his side, just as more red lights came through existing holes, and another jagged barb thrust through the surface and dragged back, making a thumb-sized hole. It would have gone right through his guts if he hadn't moved. Weighty footsteps below, moving off the landing and into his bedroom, and another hole punched from there. The attic floor was being scored by them; each one a possible seeing- or hearing-hole, or whatever the red lights meant. Another. The thing had long arms to reach up so high. This time it rattled the spike around, tore off a chunk of floor, there was a clatter of plaster below. If this continued it could perforate the floor enough to pull it apart; and if it got lucky it might stab them before that.

Maggie screamed as a spike punched up near where her hand rested on the floor.

"Against the wall!" Callum whispered, hoping to bide time.

More crunching of plaster and wood: it seemed to be working on the hole above their bed. Other noises downstairs, probably more of them coming in. Callum ran to a skylight, swivelled it open on its central hinge. From here it felt like the roiling clouds were right above his head, smoky and thick with heat, like being in an oven. The roof fell at a sharp pitch, a straight slide to the gutter and a drop of two floors to the gravel path around the house. Too much. The nearest tree too far to jump to. More explosions of plaster and aggressive crunching at the floor behind him, and barely-suppressed whimpers from the kids. The garden below could be full of these creatures still. He didn't want to go down there. But the frenzied tearing at the attic floor was far too effective. More things crashing downstairs, as if they were trashing the house, looking for anyone hiding. Thorough. He was thankful he hadn't suggested concealing themselves under a bed or in a wardrobe.

The hole was a jagged rip about a foot across, dust motes floating above it, torn yellow insulation stuck out like a dying teddy bear's fluff, metallic spike bashing away another loose part, and then something hooked over the edge. Callum rushed forward, hoped he wouldn't get spiked from below, and saw that the groping *bits* were finger-like but inhuman and red-blistered; he hammered at them with his makeshift club, putting all his fury into it as they flexed and pulled, gripping hard as they lifted something heavy from below. Callum's stick splintered but he carried on hitting, could tell the end was slick with gore yet the thing seemed able to ignore it, and now a face of some kind was rising towards him, shredded and partially skinned, threaded with red-slicked metal pieces; another set of hooked claws grabbed the floor edge and pulled, using the leverage to force that head through the gap, twitching and widening it with its body as Callum pounded on its skull; Callum yelled and thrust the sharp end of his broken cudgel into what seemed to pass for reddened eyes on the thing. It scrabbled for him angrily, he stabbed again despite feeling sick to his stomach, plunging through gore and snapping the end off his stick, leaving it protruding from the ruined semblance of a face; the thing gave an electronic screech, lips not moving, noise from some other part he didn't want to think about ... and it fell, tearing a chunk of floor away, all landing on the bed which collapsed from the sounds of it. That creature was incredibly heavy. And now the hole was bigger than before. Maybe big enough for it to fit through on a second attempt.

Weird sounds from below, inhumanly guttural and electronic, more than one; presumably getting ready for another assault. Callum glanced from the broken flooring to the holes beneath his feet, then ran back to the skylights. He opened the one furthest to the left, had to really yank on it because it was so stiff from disuse. So little time to think, ever since the chase from the barn. He leaned out. This was the back of the house nearest the side of the building; he knew that just to the left when you reached the gutter there was a drainpipe. An old one, metal, not the crappy plastic kind; as far as he knew it was securely fixed to the wall. It could take a man's weight, he hoped.

There was no going through the house, no staying. He glanced at his family. Only Cerys looked back at him, eyes wide, arms clutched round Michael and Maggie. Cerys feared heights. He just had to hope she was more scared of the things below.

"Here, now!" he said, taking the belt off his jeans. "I'll lower you out, one at a time. Once your feet are on the gutter go to your right a bit. Climb down the drainpipe. You can do it. I'll follow."

"I can't!" said Cerys, looking out the other skylight.

"You've got to!" Callum snapped.

"I'll go first." It was Maggie. She was shaking.

There was no time for debates. Maggie used to do gymnastics. She was stronger than she looked. Maybe if she went first it would strengthen Cerys. He helped Maggie out of the skylight; she held on to the edge, feet sloping down. Then he got her to wrap the end of the belt round her hand and grip tight. He leaned out, lowered her, muscles aching as he gripped his end of the belt, counteracting the slippery sweat. The window's frame cut into his bare chest. Michael and Cerys watched from the other skylight. From the corner of his eye he saw a red light flicker up through the hole in the attic floor, blink out. Maggie's feet were on the gutter, and she let go of the belt, kept her body flat against the 45 degree roof, edged her way along, and he prayed that the gutter was strong enough: he was putting her life into his panic-born idea. Movement in the rooms below, like something being dragged. Maggie squatted, lowered one leg then the other, hips above the drainpipe; she gripped the gutter and lowered the rest of her body.

"Easy," she whispered, and smiled at Callum. Something of confidence there. Pride surged through him, and despite it all he smiled back as her face disappeared from view.

Callum looked at Cerys.

"I'll go last," she said, weakly.

"No, Mum, you go next," Michael said, pushing her towards Callum. "Me and Dad can do it easy."

Good lad. If she was last, she'd never do it.

"Don't argue. You need to get down there and look out for Maggie. Be ready for Michael when he comes down. They need you to. *I* need you." His hand on her arm was firm, as reassuring as he could muster.

She climbed through the gap, teeth gritted but determined. And a resemblance between her and Maggie that he'd never seen before.

Scratching over in the corner. He didn't want to look, didn't want to see one of the things halfway into the attic. It would only make it harder.

"You can do it, *cariad*."

She kissed him, held the belt, he leaned out as before, expecting her to be heavier than Maggie but she wasn't. Stiffer with tension, but she must have lost weight. A twinge of guilt that he hadn't noticed. But he was glad of her lightness as he leaned further out of the skylight to compensate for her lack of agility. He had to be quicker, stretched, ignored the pain in his arms and chest, felt Michael gripping his legs and holding on so Callum could reach further, "Hurry!" Callum told her, because there was a creak of wood from nearby and he couldn't tell if it was in the attic or below it, couldn't look – if it came to it he'd boost Michael out and just hope he could do it alone while Callum held off whatever might soon be breathing down his neck ...

Cerys let go of the belt and edged along. Callum pulled back, exhausted, turned to face the attic, but the only shape there was Michael.

"It's gone quiet," Michael whispered. "Maybe they've gone?"

Callum thought of his wife and daughter outside. If the things were gone from *here*, they could be heading *there*. But why'd they give up so easily? Callum started stamping, crashing his wellies against the floor to make noise, ready to leap back if any sharp barbs ripped through the floor again ... but there was nothing. Callum shouted, "I'm up here you fuckheads!" with as much confidence as he could, stomping around to get their attention, bring them this way ... and still nothing.

"Err, Dad ..." said Michael, lying on his stomach and peering down into the biggest hole.

Callum joined him, squatted and gazed over the edge. Michael pointed. Something small, on the ruins of the bed. A rugby-ball-sized blob that pulsed, apparently composed of metal and flesh. It expanded and contracted as if breathing; like a segmented tin can crossed with a leaking maggot; and it had lights on it. Red specks; blue line flashes sometimes.

They'd gone, and left this below the hole. A part that fell off the one he'd stabbed? Didn't make sense. No, it felt like something they'd left on purpose. The timing, the placing, their absence.

"We need to go. Now," Callum said, dragging Michael to the skylight, squatting and hooking his fingers so Michael could put a foot there and climb out. Michael didn't argue. He was up, scrambled through the window, seizing the belt Callum thrust at him. Callum leaned as far as he dared, clenching his teeth against the pain cutting into him from the repeated efforts of taking another person's weight; Michael moved smoothly, got his feet on the gutter, let go. Cerys was out of sight, hopefully most of the way down the drainpipe. Callum dropped the belt, climbed out the skylight himself, rotated round so only his fingertips held it. Let go, started sliding towards the edge, a wave of panic as he imagined the two-storey drop onto leg-breaking concrete; but after a second his wellies caught the gutter, and although it rattled worryingly, it stopped him from falling. Michael was already on the drainpipe, a nimble monkey, making it look far easier than Callum knew it would be.

Callum was getting ready to lower himself onto the waste pipe when there was a sudden movement below, followed by a sickening thud and a female shriek. Someone had fallen.

He nearly fell too; hands already slick with perspiration, little to grip on to, and his heavy body tired. The shock of that thud jolted him, he slid, feet unable to get purchase, hands only stopping at the bracket that held the drainpipe to the wall, a bracket which was coming loose and tore the skin of his arm as he scraped past it; and it was as if there was no break in time from the shriek to his descent before he was at the bottom, kneeling by Cerys, the kids trying to help her up.

"She was just below me, fell near the bottom," Michael explained, as if worried he'd done something wrong.

"I'm okay," she told them. "Stop fussing." But she winced as she stood, seemed to have hurt her back.

"We've got to go." Callum eyed the yard and orchard warily, but it was the only way if they were to get away from the house in a hurry.

Maggie put her arm around Cerys, helped her hobble towards the trees, both barefooted. Michael followed, and Callum's eyes darted left and right, expecting something to charge at them from the murky shadows all around. The trees; the dense sea-blueness of the low sky; the leaf-strewn earth below; he felt trapped, enclosed. A mouse surrounded by predators. He saw nothing that could be a weapon. Held his bleeding arm against his chest, which became sticky with the sweat and blood. He'd live.

They'd just entered the trees when it hit them. Michael was flung to the floor; Callum staggered into a tree; Maggie and Cerys fell to their knees. Leaves showered them as the treetops rocked back then righted themselves. Pieces of glass flew past from the house's windows while the concussion blast reached out in every direction, crackling with charge, pinging off bodies and bark alike. Callum looked back at the house – it still stood, appeared the same as before apart from the shattered windows like empty eye sockets watching his family. It wasn't hard to imagine real eyes looking out at them from the darkness within.

"Get up, keep going," he commanded hoarsely.

They did. For a few steps. Then Michael fell. Seemed to have trouble getting up, Callum had to help him.

"Dad, my leg isn't working right."

Maggie and Cerys continued towards deeper cover, good. "What is it?" he asked his son.

"I can't feel anything in my leg, it tingles ... and my arm!"

An edge of fear to his voice. Callum checked him quickly but could see no wounds, nothing obvious. Whatever the blast did, it wasn't like a normal bomb, or there'd be more damage to the house. Callum remembered the skin-prickling charge that had spread out, maybe it did something to nerves? They'd all been behind trees apart from Michael on the right. It suddenly made sense: the things clearing out, the blast – and that gave him hope. If the things assumed they were all now paralysed in the attic they'd head back up there to get them, kill them, eat them, whatever. Maybe this had bought them some time after all, and the things weren't about to spring a trap in the orchard.

Callum picked Michael up, flung him over his shoulder in a fireman's lift, and staggered into the trees, out of sight of the house's blank eyes, hoping he was quick enough. Caught up with Maggie and Cerys. They had veered off, were heading to the pumpkin field, which was a vast expanse of muddy openness that would bog them down and make them visible.

"Stop!"

He lowered Michael, careful of his limbs. "Don't worry," he whispered to his son. "It was just a ... stun blast." Was that a thing? He didn't know. But Michael smiled, as if understanding, and relieved. He believed Callum.

They all squatted down low. Cerys seemed to notice Michael's problem for the first time, stroked his face.

"I'll be fine, Mum. Just stunned."

"What are we going to do, Dad?" asked Maggie. Callum noted that they were all turning to him, expecting him to have answers, rather than turning to him as if he was the obstacle for once. He couldn't let them down.

"I think we need to get away from here. No point hiding. They're fast so we can't outrun them on foot. We could get to the car, but the keys are in the house."

They looked at him with terror, Cerys began to shake her head.

"Don't worry, that's not my plan. They're probably heading back into the house; and I have a feeling that whatever happened to the electrics would stop the car working too. I think we should get the bikes." The good old family bicycles. Bought with plans for household outings, picnics, laughing faces and sunny lanes; doomed to disuse by arguments, the intruding business of work, and a cold wetness that hung over the hills more days than not. "They don't have electrics. If we follow the trees we'll be out of sight; then sneak round the outbuildings to the bike shed, grab the cycles. From there we can get on the back lane, leave this place behind."

"But Michael can't walk!" Cerys pointed out.

"I'll give him a backie."

Michael grinned.

They set off straight away. Had only gone a few yards when there was a tremendous screeching sound from the house, an echo picked up by other grating voices that seemed half static, half needle dragged across a record. Behind them, yes; but they knew their victims had got away. And now they'd come looking.

"Hurry," Callum urged.

"Hey, Dad," Michael whispered to him, only just audible above the pounding in Callum's head. "I think I'm getting feeling back."

Callum set him down, relieved to give up his son's weight for a moment. Michael moved his arm; raised the leg and wobbled it.

"It started tingling, like pins and needles. It's getting better. Just a stun blast, like you said." And there was a look of wonder there; respect. His dad had surprised him, grown in stature to the figure a little boy saw. Callum pulled him in, hugged him strongly, too hard maybe but Michael didn't complain. Then arm's length.

"Can you walk?"

Michael took a step. Cerys and Maggie were watching, crouching next to a nearby tree.

"Yes."

"Good lad. I'm proud of you." More screeching sounds echoing around the farm. How many of the things were there? Too many. And not all the sounds came from the house. Clattering crashes from one of the outbuildings now. They were out, and looking. And seemed to be exactly where he needed to take his family. One thing that was true in these hills, Da's favourite saying: it never rains, but it pours.

"Go with your mum. Get to the outbuildings and all three of you hide behind the oil tank. I'll be there in a minute."

"What are you doing?"

"Getting us more time."

He didn't wait. Moved away from them, tree to tree. Ears alert to any sound. Damp leaves slushing underfoot. The blue pulses in the clouds let him glance at his arm, the blood showing up as black streaks. It was clotting. The blood on his chest looked like war paint. So be it.

Back to near the house, the sheltered wood pile. The logs were too short to be much use but there were buckets there. He ignored the plastic ones, snatched up the old metal pail. Too light to go far. He scrambled around on his hands and knees, fingers squishing into cold and rotten windfall, dropped the squashy fruit into the bucket, feeling things crawl on his hands: earwigs, or harvestmen. A third of a bucket. Noises even in the orchard. Couldn't be cut off. This had to work. Heavy enough. He got as near to the house as he dared without stepping into full view. He was near the old outhouse with the washing machine. On the other side of that was where the car was parked. Out of sight, and just about the furthest point from the bike shed, which was way on the other side of all the farm buildings. Perfect. He held the curved wire handle, swung the bucket, got enough momentum to take it in a 360 degree circle, round and round at his side, up and down, and as his aching arm swung forward and up the last time he let go, watched the weighted bucket fly up and over the outhouse, rewarding him a few seconds later with a crash and rattle, possibly even scraping the car; the echo of the rolling bucket grinding in its final ever-decreasing circle was the only sound. The other noises in the farm had stopped. He imagined ears, or whatever their equivalent was, listening eagerly. A guttural grinding from somewhere; a popping hiss of feedback elsewhere; movement. Towards the trusty bucket's resting place. Away from his family.

Towards Callum.

He retreated, staying low, avoiding the most obvious line from the outbuildings and trying to keep as many trees around him as possible. Who knew what kind of vision these things had? Once again, he'd created time. Not enough, but there never *was* enough. That was life. It would have to do.

Luckily the ground was so damp that twigs bent and split silently rather than cracking sharply like in the hard heart of winter. He was quiet enough that he heard it coming before it heard him. Felt a vibration through his feet, footsteps, pounding meaning it was either quick or moving on all fours; Callum stood straight, back to one of the older apple trees just in time. A few feet behind him it slowed. A noise like breathing, or the artificial respirator one of his aunts had used in the dim past; Callum held his own breath. A red light glinted, laser pointer winking amongst the trees, blinked out. His neck prickled as if he was being watched. Uncertain movements, maybe the thing was turning. Could it smell him? The sweat drenching Callum's body had to be giving off pheromones. And he could certainly smell that thing, like hot oil from an over-worked engine crossed with the stench of an animal market, those hateful places Da used to take him to where all the sounds were to do with money or hopelessness, depending on which species made them. It had given him nightmares. No wonder he switched to crops, even though the subsidies seemed ten times less and work seemed ten times harder.

A horse-like snort, closer. Callum dared not move a muscle, let alone edge further round the tree. He'd just have to hope it didn't come any nearer, discover him cowering weak-kneed against the rough bark. Then there was a squeal in the distance, and immediately the footsteps – or maybe even hoofbeats – pounded away again, towards the house. No time to wait for full safety, Callum planted his lips on the tree's bark, kissed it, and moved on towards the outbuildings. "Please let them be safe," he chanted, inaudible to any but himself.

WHEELS

He got through the orchard with no more trouble. His knees were stiff from all the crouching down, but that didn't matter. Only getting away mattered. Getting them all away from this madness, this nightmare taking place in the thin layer squished between blue Hell sky and hard ground.

As he approached the outbuildings he eyed the barn with distrust, remembering what had happened in there, and was surprised to realise it couldn't have been much more than half an hour ago this all started. It felt like he'd lived a year since then.

The creepy blue light from the sky meant he could run without bumping into walls; it was enough to see by. The equivalent of a full moon night. The oil tank cast a large shadow. He had to assume his family were there. He couldn't see anyone wedged into that gap between tank and wall, but that was a good thing.

Getting to the tank required a sprint across the open. The noises seemed further away. Hopefully they all teemed in one place. No strange lights, smells, hints of movement here.

Couldn't wait any longer. He dashed across the gap, not looking left or right, just aiming at the shelter. Safety.

Then again, those shadows were deep. He hoped it was safety he was running into, and not the twitching arms of something *alien*.

"Hello?" he whispered.

"Callum!" Cerys pulled him into the greater darkness, squeezed him fiercely. He was aware of light touches from the kids. "I thought ..."

"I'm fine. Let's go."

"Maybe they've gone?" Maggie said, hopefully. "They're quiet."

"That's what I'm worried about."

They moved out in a line, Cerys insisted everyone held hands. She limped but told him it was only bruising. Callum led them away from the house, round the back of the barn, beyond the tool shed – out of sight of the worst places where the things might be watching from.

Michael reached the bike shed first. The building was leaning. Neglected and forgotten out on its own, like the things it stored in lieu of Callum making a firm decision to get rid of them. Always the hope that something would be useful later, that things could change and they'd gain a new lease of life. And right now he was glad of that.

"It's padlocked," Michael said. "Have you got a key, Dad?"

Callum tried the padlock first. Locked and rusty, as expected. If he had a crowbar he'd have it off in seconds. Instead he looked round; at the edge of the drive there were ornamental white stones, dug up and moved over years of ploughing. Callum remembered once swearing to Cerys that the rocks grew like seeds, otherwise how come there were more every year? He hefted one that was larger than his hand, it felt about right. He took a deep breath: there was no way to do this quietly. When he smashed the single cracked window of the shed Michael cringed at the noise; Callum used the rock as a hammer, working quickly to knock out jagged edges. Each one shattered on the shed's floor, seeming to break into teeny tinkling pieces just to spite him.

Without hesitating or worrying about cuts he scrambled through the frame and thudded to the wooden floor within. Bikes in a jumble, but not chained together. Any flat tyres would have to be damned. He grabbed the first bike, almost flung it out through the window where Michael and Maggie took hold of it.

"Take it and go straightaway, don't wait," Callum told them, already lifting the next bike in a creak of springy, damp floorboards. Michael nodded, held the bike for his sister. She wobbled but got going, heading off down the lane.

"Dad," said Michael, worry on his face. "There's noises coming this way."

Callum handed him the next bike. "Go."

Next was an old shopper, basket still attached. Cerys' bike from years ago. He remembered her coming back from the village with the basket full on a Saturday: newspaper, bread, a tin or two; looking so dainty and ladylike. He handed it through the window to her.

"They're getting nearer, Callum, you –"

"Just go! GO! I'm right behind you!"

She did. Callum threw the last bike, a 1970s racer, through the gap; climbed after it and ran with the bike, leapt on while it was moving, freewheeled until he gave up on trying to get the welly toes into the toe caps and just started pedalling with the straps upside down; yes, noises not far behind. A screech. Definitely after his blood. Family ahead, safer; he pedalled like mad, stood, thrusting his legs down hard to get up speed. In the sky the clouds seemed to part for a second, and he glimpsed something that had been hidden there, something of tremendous size, horrifyingly low and close, but he didn't look, didn't want to be distracted; diamond shaped beams off to his left, his right, then more ahead: one, two. Was it some way of moving the things? He went faster, wishing he had been on a cycle in the last few years and wasn't as rusty as the bike; he passed the places on each side of the lane where the beams had landed, movement in the shadows amongst the bushes there but he was past; he dared a side glance back but the bike hit a rut on the muddy surface; he wobbled, heart leaping into his mouth, heard a grating squeal from behind, a hunter on the trail, he swayed but angled it right at the last second and instead of ploughing off the path into a tree he managed to veer back into the centre of the lane. He picked up speed, pedalling like the Devil was on his heels, as Da used to say.

Why so many thoughts of his old man tonight?

It was downhill now, he went faster, felt that it was working and he was making space. Down to the junction with the road, family had reached it and gone right towards the village; Callum braked just enough to take the corner at a wide angle without hitting the fence or getting bogged in mud, then caught up with them. Took a chance to look back – nothing. Forward was clear too. Michael looked like he was smiling. Good kid. Callum knew how he felt. When the adrenalin faded he'd be exhausted, but right now he could have whooped for joy.

The road was painted with *ARAF*, "SLOW". His breath was coming so hard he didn't need telling twice. "Stop," he shouted. "Stop for a minute!"

They pulled into a layby with a squeak of brakes; he wheeled past, turned his bike to face the three of them. On one side there was a drop down to the stream. Small beginnings that would feed into Afon Ystud later. The other side was a gorse-filled hill. It looked safe enough.

"Stay on your bikes in case we need to head off again in a hurry," Callum said, loosening his death grip from the handlebars.

"Like if we're being followed, you mean?" asked Maggie, with a backward glance.

"Exactly like that. Michael – how's your arm and leg?"

Michael wiggled them. "Back to normal."

"Cerys – your back?" Callum had noted the way she was trying to keep her bum off the bike seat.

"Don't worry about me. I'm just amazed we're all here. You did it all. That was ... I don't know what to say."

They all looked at him. Confidence and trust in those eyes. It was too much. He was only being a dad and a husband. "We need to decide what to do next. Can't stay here. Can't go back."

"What about the village?" asked Cerys.

"Option one. Hope things are normal there, and we can get help."

"You don't sound convinced."

"Look up. What do you notice?"

"The weird clouds," Cerys replied after a few seconds of observation. "Blocking the sky. Blue lightning every now and again."

"I think I know what Dad means," Michael said, scanning the horizon. "The sky's the same as far as we can see. There's some clearer bits around here but it thickens up again ahead. If the cloud's anything to do with those things, then they could be anywhere. It definitely looks like a big patch over Llany."

Callum was looking back the way they'd come. Wanted to curse. They were on the clock again. Luckily, his family hadn't noticed anything.

"Could we hide here?" asked Maggie. "Leave the bikes, hide up on that hill or something?"

"Another possibility," said Callum. "But we wouldn't be able to go far. Above a narrow band. See how the clouds cling to the tops of the hills? Looks like thick smoke. Not normal." Who knew what moved in that thick blanket-like layer covering everything, what caused those blue pulses? Electricity? Baking heat? Worse monsters; things which only lived in that kind of extreme atmosphere, that hunted in impenetrable fog? The clouds, blue light and heat could be dangerous in some way. Radioactive, or germ-ridden. Things with long-term effects. There was enough to worry about right now. Callum would count himself lucky if they all survived this night.

"I vote for the town," said Michael. "Get help. Get far from the farm."

Cerys and Maggie agreed, and the four set off. Callum kept quiet about those sparkling diamond beams he'd seen at the farm, and which he'd spotted getting nearer as they talked; glowing fingers of light that dissolved when they contacted the earth. They made him think of searchlights. He rode to the rear, so he'd know immediately if any of them had bike trouble.

At one point he glanced back. Up in the clouds he noticed motion, in a few seconds when the mist swirled and cleared. A huge shape, floating, like a glimpse of a giant manta ray; or like a jellyfish, bigger than his whole farm, drifting in that blueness like an alien sea.

Maybe the lights were teleports; or maybe they were more like stingers.

Either way, it was good to move in the opposite direction.

Huw

They approached Llanwrthyl under the hot, roiling cloud, passing the outlying houses. Silent. Dark. The word "dead" sprang to mind but there was no need to jump to morbid conclusions. It was the middle of the night. It didn't mean the things were here.

They freewheeled down one of the two main streets; post office, Black Lion, chemist, butchers, optician. The street lights were off. Was that normal? Callum was deciding where they'd knock and seek help, holding back the decision due to a disturbed feeling, when they rounded a bend and he heard the first screams; smelt burning; saw broken windows. There was an explosion somewhere further into the town.

It was here too.

"Back!" he yelled, and they swung their bikes in sharp arcs, but then a body smashed through the upper window of one of the houses ahead of them; the person twisted in the air, smacked hard pavement amongst shards of glass, blood ... and something looked out the window, a distorted head, it saw them, and jerky limbs began to heave its bulk through; maybe it could climb or drop down, Callum didn't care, he turned again and led his family away and into the town, left the main street for a side road to break line of sight. The crossing lights were off too, everything was off tonight; hard right down an alley that he knew wasn't a dead end; there was a hairdresser, a café, and it was out of view of the main throughways. In the dark they might evade the thing from the window if it was chasing them and not doing whatever the fuck it meant to do to the broken body that had preceded it.

At the end of the alley there was a grating screech. Artificial. Familiar. Callum said nothing, just braked, leaned his bike against the wall and ducked behind some concrete steps leading up to Morgan's Café entrance. The kids were with him, smart enough to crouch and stay silent. He was alert for movement: maybe a flicker of curtain up above, maybe imagination. Looked back – yes, Cerys too, they were together. Finger to his lips. The inhuman screech faded, but there were other noises in the street this alley led to. Sickeningly human moans. No way back. No way on.

Again that feeling of being trapped, low clouds over a tight alley, danger everywhere, the rat feeling again, sweat trickling down his chest. Not worried for himself but for those in his care. They were in a tunnel and the terriers could appear at either end at any moment.

A motion again. Curtain? Someone watching? Callum mouthed "Help!" at the window just in case. He could try to force a way in somewhere. Break into the café. It was too exposed out here in the alley, too vulnerable.

A door opened across the way, hand gesturing urgently. Callum pointed it out and they didn't hesitate, crossed the lane, hastened into the dark hallway; relief as the door to the street closed with a click behind them.

"Thanks. We owe you," Callum told the man who'd saved them.

"What were you doing out there, you fools? Should have stayed in your house."

"We got chased out. Ty'n Froch Farm. Got away on those bikes out there."

"Follow me." He was elderly, led the way upstairs clutching the bannister. All the curtains were tightly closed, keeping dangerous darkness out ... and the safer darkness within.

Off the landing and into a small flat. Mysterious shapes resolved into a frilly-fringed floor lamp; solid armchair; cabinet of crockery; old-style fat TV. The man parted the curtains at each window as he passed, looked out, pulled them tight closed again. Actions with the nervous energy of ritual. Only when he deemed it safe did he gesture for them to sit on the sofa and chairs. Callum sighed as he lowered himself down into smothering softness, finally able to relax. He hadn't realised how exhausted he was, buoyed up on panic.

"I have candles but don't want to use them. I watched. I worked out that those things can see really well." The old man was just a shadow in the cold cobalt light flickering round the curtains. "But can I get you anything? Glass of water?"

"That would be lovely," said Cerys. "*Diolch*."

"So the mains is still on?" Callum asked.

"That, and gas. No light though. No juice from the plug sockets. No telly, no radio, no phone. No police or army, either."

"You been in the whole time?"

"Yes. Woke up when it started, dripping in sweat, noises out there. I thought it was a riot at first. A riot in Llany! That'd be something new for old eyes. Thought I was having a nightmare."

The man filled glasses, handed them out. Callum's throat had been dry as baked mud. After a few gulps he introduced himself and his family; found out the old guy was called Huw.

"What do you think they are?" Maggie asked the old man whilst stifling a yawn. The poor kids seemed more tired than Callum was.

"Easy. Devils. Well, that or aliens, but I think they're from Hell. Look all burnt, don't they? Tortured. You get a good look when they're dragging us away."

"What do you mean?" asked Callum, leaning forward. He'd not had a chance to reflect on what they might want.

"Not seen it? They drag the bodies off. Doesn't seem to matter if you're alive or dead. Some of them are stunned, get put into weird bags, like thick clear plastic. I saw someone trying to escape from one, panicking, looked like they were screaming but I couldn't hear them through the material, whatever it is. They all get dragged off and the devils come back for more. Not just people, neither. Saw one dragging a dog by its tail. Half the dog's head was gone, smearing brains down the road – oh, sorry," the man said, seeing Maggie's face.

Dogs. Cats. People. Callum's chickens. So they wanted animals. Flesh and bones.

"It makes no sense. Them taking us." Callum ran hands over the stubble on his chin.

"It's like when your crops're ripe," Michael said. They were all thinking about the implications when Michael added: "What if it's not just here? What if it's all over the world, and there's nowhere safe to go?"

There were a few seconds of silence before Cerys told him not to scare his sister.

The thought scared Callum too. He needed the distraction of practicalities.

"When they drag bodies away, where do they take them?"

Callum was just thinking aloud, but Huw said, "Vicarage Fields."

"Huh?"

"That's where they go. All head in that direction with the bags and the bits. The playing field by the river. I reckon that's where they have their nest. Or burrow. Or hole to Hell. All go that way, then come back for more."

The old man peered through his curtains again. "Speaking of which – I think we're going to have to leave."

"Why?" Callum couldn't keep the exasperation out of his voice. Seeing his family safe wasn't something he was ready to relinquish.

"Because they're coming down the road. Searching house by house. I can see 'em at the end – the only reason they've not got me is because they haven't searched here yet. That's how I know they're not animals. This is organised. It's – military."

"What's the point of leaving?" Callum persisted. "There's no safety out there. Maybe we'd be better off defending than running."

The old man shook his head. "I saw them break into a building. Took them seconds. The people in there ..." He exhaled through pursed lips, like a dying breeze. "But I don't mean just run randomly. From here I could see a lot of the searching. Thing is, there's areas they've searched already. Once you've secured an area you don't waste time hanging around if there's other targets nearby. So we cross the road, make our way through the clock yard, get to somewhere behind Cwm Lodge, hole up in one of the houses there, keep quiet. That's a chance. Staying here – we'd have half an hour, if that."

The old guy wasn't panicking. A cool head in a cardigan. Much as Callum hated going out again, he believed. There was no question in his mind about the right thing to do.

"What do you think?" Callum asked his family.

During the flurry of preparations Cerys examined Callum's arm at the sink, ignoring his protest. Cleaned and sterilised it, used a plaster from Huw's old metal first aid box. The cut wasn't bad. Being namby-pambied was the bit Callum hated, but it seemed to calm Cerys. This was for her.

Huw found some shorts for Maggie to wear under her baggy T-shirt, and old trainers that almost fit when she combined them with a few pairs of socks; he'd also dug out some sandals for Cerys.

Now Huw threw Callum a shirt to cover his bare torso. Callum held it up near the window. Flowery with a big collar.

"From the '70s," Huw explained. "You wouldn't fit the shirts I wear now, but back then I was bigger. All muscles and spunk."

The kids sniggered as they peeped out the window. They used to laugh together a lot when they were younger, before Maggie declared she was too old to play with Michael any more.

"Ready to try for it?" asked Huw, gathering something up with a clink of glass.

"I think so. What's that?"

"Molotovs. Whisky that's been sat in the cupboard for donkey's years. Probably lethal by now."

Callum sniffed the cloth rag stuck from the top. "Whew, strong all right," he said. "Almost seems a waste. How come you never drank it?"

"Christmas presents off my brother-in-law while my wife was alive. He hates me and I hate whisky." Huw flicked his lighter, testing it with a flame for a second that gave a welcome orange glow to the room. "Wish it was him in this town, instead of me."

Flame out, back to blue.

Lost

The road was hard on his face; grazed and throbbing, he turned and looked along the ground's perspective at the burning house beyond, orange flames scorching the night up in a colour other than blue for the first time in forever. Head ringing, maybe concussion, but he had to stand and forced himself to lurch up; it took two attempts after jelly limbs dropped him back to painful solidity on the first try. A scream cut through the grogginess, blurred movement, staggering and leaning on each other, a family ... they were his. Follow. Heat of flames behind, more screams, panic and pain combined, Huw on fire, bumping into a wall again and again as his hair and face melted, clothes fusing to body in a stench, and things beyond trying to get to him but put off by the scorching heat, or the brightness. Nothing he could do. Huw was gone. Callum remembered: ambush, Huw threw one bomb, the other exploded on him when a creature got close and lashed out, and maybe one of their stun bombs or blasts would explain having no real memory of the chaos following. For now he just stumbled away from the pool of flames at his back, followed the direction of the others, trying to work feeling back into limbs. Up some steps and past a phone box, a stone memorial, sitting area, towards the figures in the blue darkness ahead; "Wait," but it came out as a croak, he crawled up the steps on hands and knees, vision swimming but resolving into two figures, Michael, Cerys, and she cursed and shouted while Michael tried to drag her away, "Where's Maggie? Where's my daughter?" she yelled.

Callum went back alone, saw Huw being pulled away in metallic talons, his body smoking, crisped and raw, hopefully dead. Two others were holding down a struggling figure; one of them raised something, a rod, a weapon, bifurcated and jagged; the figure was swallowed up in a white sheet, skin, plastic that enfolded and contracted like vacuum-packed meat, took away the sealed person, and he knew it was Maggie, he *knew* it, but there were at least four of the things by the dying flames. Another appeared, pulling a blood-soaked carcass by its hair, part of the leg missing and a trail of darkness followed.

Maggie was gone.

It would be suicide to run out there now. He bit down on his tongue, hard, and tasted coppery blood before he returned to the ones he still had, the ones he needed to get to safety.

Vows

"We've got to!" Cerys' hands twitched. Callum knew if he could see her face clearly it would be tear-lined and ferocious.

"We're not," Callum replied, as gently but firmly as he could.

He'd had to half-drag her to get her here to the church. In the area beyond where the aliens were searching, to a place the creatures had been already. Huw mustn't have been the only one with that plan. The lanky vicar had let them through a gap in the barricade of benches. Children being comforted by surrogate parents; lovers hugging on long seats; an old couple knelt and prayed in the near-darkness. Almost everyone in their nightwear, ripped from slumber and normality. Michael was sleeping on one of the seats, had conked out almost as soon as they got to safety. Whispers ceased and eyes turned to Cerys, whose voice disrupted the delicate signals they were sending to their god.

Would morning never come?

"We can't leave her! She's my daughter! You fucking coward! Just standing there!" She tried to pass him, he stepped in front of her again.

Cerys renewed her attack. "Just as long as your favourite is safe, eh?"

"No, it's –"

"We've got to try, got to see. You don't love her, you never did."

"No, I –"

And she slapped him. Hard. The sound of it echoed in the vast space. It hurt because he'd never raised a hand to her, nor she to him; one of the things he'd seen and would never do. The vicar hurried over to complain about the noise, Cerys worrying people.

Callum ignored him. Just looked into Cerys' eyes. "You're wrong," he told her, quietly.

"Liar! You'll let her die because you're an emotionless bastard, a dead husband, and you might not love her but I *do*!"

"I'm not a liar. I'm going after her. Always was."

She stared at him, taking in his stoic calm, and then sank onto the carpeted step behind her, face on hands, chest heaving with sobs like he'd never wanted to see. He'd rather endure meanness than see her hurting so much her spirit broke.

He knelt. Kneaded her shoulder with one clumsy hand until she looked up.

"She's alive. She's alive, Cerys. They put her in a bag. They only do that with the living. I promise I'll do all I can to get her back. You were wrong. I do love her."

"Oh God, I'm sorry!"

Quieter now. The vicar left. Survivors went back to praying. It was just Cerys and Callum, like the old days.

"I had to get you two safe first. There's time."

There never had been enough before: please let tonight be the exception.

"You shame me. I should go. I gave birth to her!"

He considered her. She was brave through the fear. Brave and beautiful.

He almost said, "No, if it doesn't work out then you'd be a better parent to Michael than I would. You always were." But he knew she'd just argue. So instead he told her, "I've got a better chance of getting her back. I'm stronger. And I can't just sit by and wait. Can't risk losing both of you in one night."

He was in a church and they said religion was for miracles: Cerys didn't argue.

"In sickness and in health," he whispered as he left.

MAGGIE

The sky seemed to throb above the playing field, blue clouds swirling low with an electrical hum; the area was lit in the otherworldly blue of a gas flame, an idea reinforced by the sweltering heat, worse than working fields in summer sun.

The monsters had been piling bodies. Some were in bags, others the unresisting dead; and some were just parts, torn limbs and broken torsos. He'd watched for a few minutes from the bushes by the river. Drag, dump, return to the town for more. Meanwhile others placed bodies and parts into lines which seemed to rise, float, as if on some invisible mechanical slope which ran up into the oily clouds. He knew what was there now. The clouds had parted for a second in some shift of air current and he'd seen the craft drifting – or rather, a section of the craft, a curved black underbelly that glistened like slug skin. He'd only seen part of the whole. The ship was enormous, terrifyingly awesome, awful, giving the impression of a landmass above, flipping perceptions so it appeared *below*, something you fell towards, basalt rock that wanted to crush you. Everything was being sucked up into that mass.

Fewer and fewer bodies were lined up. The process was slowing. Ending. Time running out before the next stage, whatever that was.

He'd had a few minutes to study the invaders. Their limbs bent in gruesome ways, joints only an approximation of the beings on Earth, like jigsaw pieces forced to fit by adding gaps and teeth in brute-force puzzle solving. Yet they were quick and agile, improvements on us: melting into lines of poor visibility, deeper shadow, obstacles; displaying predator mindsets with their whole beings.

The ones lining up bags had finished. No more parts, no more townsfolk. There wouldn't be a better opportunity. He crouched and crossed the deadly open ground to the gruesome conveyor. Even up close there was no physical belt or escalator, it seemed to be done with hard light, and he felt the pull on his skin as he edged round the risers, trying to check those awaiting that fate, those in bags.

He realised the people within were conscious. Sealed in tight, thick plastic, tapering to welded tube-like ends. They were muffled but many were trying to scream, as if suffocating. A woman, not Maggie, trying to scratch her way out but unable to get purchase for her broken fingernails, sliding on a slippery interior; and she saw him, was more frantic in her efforts to escape this alien prison.

He hesitated. Knew he should check the other body bags as quickly as possible, find Maggie; yet couldn't stand the thought of leaving someone's mother, someone's daughter; how he'd feel if Maggie was left to die by a rescuer focussed only on their own kin.

He wore a tool belt looted from a hardware store on the way here, stepping through a smashed shop window in crunches of glass and gathering anything that might help. Hammer, crowbar, screwdriver. He removed a Stanley knife, clicked out the triangular blade, knelt and started cutting. He'd expected it to slice easily but it was like sawing through a thick plastic milk carton with a butter knife. Fine cross-strands reinforced the greasy-feeling membrane; the woman realised what he was doing, held still, but it could take minutes ... and there was motion coming as some of the creatures were returning with another haul. It couldn't be done. He mouthed "Sorry", and she panicked again as he moved away, but he couldn't do it, couldn't help, only focus on the approaching *things*. He was less than twenty feet from where the bodies rose up, lifted in the invisible talons; he would be seen. He knelt beside a broken body, no head, a man, chest punctured and holes leaking gore; Callum scooped as much as he could, still warm, rubbed it on his arms and face; threw himself down beside the corpse. Eyes tight shut. He heard the movement as the broken-flesh beasts lined up their catch. Then he felt a pull on his clothes, hair, skin; his gut twisted as he rose, nothing below him but the imprint of wet grass.

His stomach churned. Never liked heights. Looked down once at the receding ground, the nothingness that lifted him further from his home, sucked him up into a nightmare, a world turned upside down in one night. He closed his eyes tight again.

Weight returned to his body, stomach settling down amongst internal organs that had shifted as if separated by unseen fingers. The sound quality was different. Not the outdoor fade-away, but enclosed in hardness so even breathing seemed to echo back at you, unable to escape and become one with the sky. A shell of confinement. He was moving but horizontally now, somehow more normal as if pressed onto floor, sliding gently on a polished surface that smelt of unnameable chemicals, like pesticide, damp artificial fertiliser, evaporating oil. He opened his eyes and had to squint as they adjusted to the new brightness.

A curving hall. Lined in a smooth-looking surface with frozen ridges rippling along it, resembling the way networked veins push up old skin. The light came from filaments which threaded along them. He couldn't even describe the colour. Indigo? Mauve? Amethyst? A cross between neon glow and organic suffusion; the hippy flowers on his shirt shone as if under UV lights in a nightclub (hazy memories of another lifetime). His temples throbbed, something to do with how the light strained his eyes.

Or maybe it was the '70s shirt, seen clearly for once.

The floor was the same surface as the walls and ceiling, one long curved tube apart from a narrow strip of pulsing blue that seemed to have no moving parts yet transported the line of bodies along. No smears – even bloodied torsos moved neatly, as if not fully in contact with the glowing surface. Looking back, Callum couldn't see a start or end to it, how they'd entered the ship – only a moving line of bodies and bags that curved sharply out of sight. Then they stopped moving. Sudden, but without the jolt of something mechanical.

The conveyor line had stilled but in the passage behind there was movement. He saw the outline of one of the things. It stoop-walked, jerky limb movements that still somehow implied fluidity, an alien perception of economy, or something badly copied. The creature was prodding at some bodies with a sharp-looking barbed bayonet of a hand, ignoring others. Its head hung low as if too heavy for the narrow neck which jutted out, and it swung suddenly in Callum's direction. He closed his eyes, not too tight, too obvious; played dead, tried to slow his breathing even though his heart resisted, raced, telling him to run too. The thing's hefty feet thumped along the line and he felt it in his body, the mass getting closer, its painful-looking inspections almost at him. He hoped he lay like a corpse. His body ached from the way his arm and head were twisted – hopefully that uncomfortable position would disguise him. As a child he'd sometimes played a game called Dead Man with his sister. One of them would pretend to be dead, a corpse discovered by a great detective, or inspected by a vampire. You had to stop breathing and make no response if prodded experimentally, or breath tickled your neck. Callum's sister often betrayed herself with nervous giggles or a squeal, but Callum could keep up the unresisting stillness for the count of sixty required to win.

The prize then was just the opportunity to boast. The stakes from playing the game with this ponderous combination of flesh and metallic parts were much higher.

He stilled everything. Concentrated on his core. But was still aware of every sensation, every sound. Behind him was a human in one of the fleshy sacks, and it struggled, fought against its confinement, a muffled and ineffectual resistance. The bulky reverberations with each footstep from this creature – which must have been as heavy as a small car – left an impression in his mind. And he felt the heat of its breath, the sour smell that came with it as it gusted over him, a smell of carrion in the heat of an over-worked engine. His hair blew back and he knew it must have lowered its head to his face. He expected to be prodded, stabbed, dragged; yet he betrayed nothing in his body, kept the muscles relaxed, expressionless, the slackness of dead tissue. The faintest sound, like motors, flywheels, cables; it was so close he could imagine obscene inner workings. Something touched him; another; tentative touches, the tip of fingers except they seemed smaller, more flexible, sharper. Something from its mouth? Then there was a scrape, metallic hooves on plating, and the stench faded to the cloying background smell of blood, as the thing moved along the line.

Callum waited until its lumbering movements had faded, the only sound being weakening struggles, thrum of vibration in the ground. He opened his eyes.

The area seemed safe at the moment. He rolled off the blue and onto the floor's surface, stood with protesting joints from the forced stillness. Saw the black bloodstains on his arms and clothes from the hasty disguise. The line began moving again. The bodies slid on; he didn't.

Instead he made his way along the line, briefly checking each body, each human struggling with confinement, just a second to be sure it was not Maggie, then on. No point trying to be stealthy since there was nowhere to hide, and he had wasted enough time. It was all or nothing now.

The gruesome conveyor moved slowly, but it still forced him to run along to keep ahead of it, try to check everyone, everything. Maggie had been taken before he got there, could be well along the line by now, wherever it led, whatever it meant. It was taking too long. He started skipping past dead bodies that were unlikely to be her; only glanced at the panicked and struggling prisoners in rubbery sacks. He scanned twenty, forty, sixty ... the line continued around a curve. He'd known the ship was huge, this would be a tiny part of its circumference. It could go on for miles. He had to fight to quell panic. How many hundreds, thousands were there?

He worked along the lines of horror. Guts. Something fused together, charred feathers amidst the redness. A bag with a human in, who wasn't struggling. A leg, torn along the thigh. A small white sack, with a baby, which didn't move, and another fleshy sack that just seemed to contain dark blood which rippled in the transportation. A teenager, male. A dead sheep, tongue lolling from a broken mouth. Dead and alive, all in demand, his mind was numbed by it, only focussing on one thing, one person who mattered beyond the others, horrible as the line of suffering was.

He blinked hard but couldn't get the images from his mind. Looked ahead at how much more sickening horror he would have to face. And saw that the corridor was turning more sharply. Maybe it spiralled in. He also noticed something he'd missed – faint circular patterns in the walls sometimes. Easy to mistake for the venous texturing in this eye-straining unnatural light, but once spotted he instinctively knew they were doors. It probably explained why he hadn't caught up with the creature that had been checking the line. The doors were just a distraction though: if Maggie was here then she was on the glowing line that moved people along. No point worrying about what might step out ahead of him, behind him, next to him.

He felt like he'd checked hundreds. He'd seen dead teenage girls; seen some still alive in bags; one had frozen him with hope, a girl, curled up and still, eyes tight shut as if refusing to look at what enclosed her. But it wasn't Maggie. He focussed on the T-shirt, bare legs, used those signs as a way of scanning victims more efficiently. His neck and head ached.

Another sharper curve, and the corridor was different, an archway studded with organic-looking domes, fist sized. He entered a cavernous room. The line of light continued, curved and bent back on itself. He was able to glance left and right, bodies moving away and towards him; leaped over the line, checked other lanes, sometimes missing out corpses and bags in his hurry to cover ground. There were hundreds more, a curving system that transported them round this huge room, ceiling so high he couldn't see it. And he became aware of a noise, snapping, rattling, like wheels on a cart that was pushed too fast over uneven paving stones. No, not quite. Scan left, scan right, follow the curve, more lanes. Or was it a slapping noise, like his hand playfully smacking Cerys' arse as she got out of the shower, making her laugh and throw her towel at him; past memory, not recent; loving palm on flesh? The lines curved again, all in this room, some kind of centre to the transportation, and the way the glowing lines moved up and down was efficient, factory-like in how they used space. He stayed stooped, checked each, apologised sometimes, and then one of the struggling bags caught his eye: maybe the extra skin visible within, or the ferocity, like a struggle of recognition, who knew? But he flung himself onto the glowing line on his knees, felt himself glide along just above the hard surface, and she saw him, recognised him through the film, saw her father. Maggie's face was mucus-stained, childlike from crying, but he cut away at the bag, ignored the noises getting louder around him, just sawed away with his small blade, saying, "It's okay, I'm here, Dad's here." The stuff was industrially-tough, his arm tired from sawing, his palm ached from gripping, but he made his first incision through the sickeningly skin-like pouch. Immediately its clutching, vacuum-like seal was broken and air got in, creating space; he could now hear Maggie's voice, saying nothing but "Dad!", sobbing with panic and relief, almost loud enough to fade out the mechanical noises which were getting louder, and amongst them something that might have been a muffled scream. Cut. Cut. They moved along together, he would stay no matter what. He felt the sliminess that sealed his daughter within. The noise was nearer. A few lines away, their destination after they'd swept to and from the curved exterior wall a few more times. He cut carefully but looked up. And saw what the noise was.

It wasn't a gentle smack of flesh. Not wheels. It was clacking.

The conveyor of people and parts moved through an arching structure, like a ribcage framework. Within he could see skeletal arms that ended in clattering beak-like points, moving rapidly, connecting parts, apparently breaking down and stitching up whatever passed through. He knew that noise now. Cerys' sewing machine.

The screams were from the living as they were cut and re-formed, the bags split open, apparently stitched onto and into them, resource and connective tissue; filaments that shone like new steel embedded and pulled taut, along with thicker rods, plates of metallic bone, reformed with new joints and parts. Burning smells as leaking parts were cauterised, blood crusted to ash, skin scarred to a shine before being sprayed, plasticated, sealed. The screaming always ended. Out the other side the line of light continued, but it was no longer the same as what had gone in. Things were fused into bigger creatures. The monsters on his farm. Each one different. Some resembling dogs, or cows, if seen through a broken kaleidoscope. Others looked more humanoid, but stretched, compressed, always in the wrong places. It was a machine. It reminded him of the grinders male chicks were thrown into on chicken farms; the struggling living reprocessed as gloopy resource.

At this point the light path he was on curved, at a close point to the flesh stitching; started to move him and Maggie away again. Two more passes and they'd be there. He realised things were getting closer together, and what had been wide gaps between the lanes of light were now so narrow you could barely see the shell-like floor's surface between them. He tried to find solid ground, something he could put a foot on, drag Maggie off to, so she'd stop moving, give him more time, but it was impossible. Like standing on a greasy slope, nowhere to get a solid foot, everywhere just curving light sliding him on; not even enough purchase to pull her to a previous line to buy more time

that way. The clacking behind him faded slightly, but they'd
be returning to it all too soon. He cut away, tried to hide the
panic. Noticed pinpoint red lights were shining on him from
somewhere. They traced his forearms, extra heat to them, but
not burning. A glance up – they came from the machine, where
a few of the beak-like limbs were extending through the gaps in
the rib frame and leaning towards him, red lights flickering on
his body, as if watching. Maybe they'd noticed he wasn't dead
or in a bag when he passed close; who knew what senses they
used? But it was obvious they were aware of him. He sawed
away, made a six inch gap and touched Maggie's fingertips for a
second in a gesture of reassurance. Then she tore at the tough and
slimy material encasing her while he worked on the other end of
the slit, trying to widen it with panicky movements. There was
something going on behind. Only a few red lights shone on him
now. He risked a look back. Alien bodies still extruded from the
framework of the stitching machine, inanimate combinations
of soft flesh and mineral hardness; but the beak-like structures
seemed to work faster on one of them. It glowed with heat and
light, and some of them seemed to stab into it, pointed needles
tracing lines up where a spine would be, up to a head, a frenzied
motion that reflected his own. He had to free her. Two more
passes. They could do it. Almost nine inches now, an arm easily,
maybe her head could fit; and there was movement, not just from
the smacking beaks, but from the thing they worked on. No
longer did they bother with multiple bodies at once, this was
pure focus on a single thing.

And, unlike the earlier ones which slid away for storage or
reanimation, this one moved.

Pushed itself to a sitting position. It was smaller than some of the ones they'd finished earlier, as if rushed. Not as heavy, not as vicious-looking. But it turned what passed for a head, faced him, and stood. The beaks were agitated, already working on another of these premature creations. The first one came into a low crouch, as if its spine didn't support it fully, or was too long, and it squeezed between two framework ribs. The light path curved. They were moving back towards the machine. One more pass. The creature would be here. Callum slipped the Stanley knife through the slit in the slimy, rubbery material, pressed it into Maggie's hand. She carried on cutting. Callum stood, balanced himself, took a hammer from the tool belt. Noted how much he was outweighed by the thing lumbering towards him. Took a screwdriver into his other hand, and moved forward, aware of Maggie's feverish sawing behind him.

It was new-born. Didn't move as firmly or confidently as the bigger ones he'd seen.

As it got nearer he noticed details that sickened him – red-blistered flesh with a gooey film on top, metal insertions threaded through. Mostly human, but a canine look to the elongated head; flaps of skin beneath the arms, as if spare, or yet to be used; and a split in the head, a horizontal gap to some internal structures he didn't want to know about.

Callum wished he had one of Huw's Molotovs to hand.

"You bastards," he said.

It raised what passed for an arm. Callum lunged forward with the hammer, hoping to strike its head, but the thing was quick; the arm fell like stone, knocked him down, shoulder stinging. He felt blood running from a cut. Rolled to the side just as it speared forward with its other limb, which ended in cruelly-barbed spikes. Callum stayed in a low crouch for better balance while the light beams beneath him moved, carrying him and the others from Earth; he noticed that the alien was not affected by the light path, seemed to pass through it and walk on the carapace-like floor beneath. Callum scrambled back across the slippy light below. It was harder for him to move with no stable surface. He risked a glance at Maggie, she was doing well, had cut a larger gap. At that second the thing struck, extending one of its arms to rake his chest, tearing open the shirt, buttons ripped off. Blood welled up from gashes. Keeping his distance was no good. Callum looked at the moving bodies, the bags, corpses; the alien was only watching him. Callum dodged to his left, and the creature turned to face him, stepped forward, got snagged on what looked like part of a cow that dripped insides onto the blue path; the alien tripped and was forced to put a hand out; it might be unaffected by the light path, but 1,000 lbs of bone and gristle counted. Callum skidded forward, raised his hammer and brought it down on the creatures head, hard, fast, again and again, forcing it to protect its jaws which dented and split along a seam of flesh and metal; dripping gore on the hammer head showed he'd hurt it, maybe they were softer when first made, like a butterfly from a chrysalis. He hoped to stove its head in but it lashed out, the blow connecting with his side, sending him sprawling. The hammer was gone, one of his ribs possibly broken. It'd happened once before, years ago, and it was the same jagged pain.

He shifted the screwdriver to his right hand. He was two lanes away from Maggie now. She was on her last pass towards the

beaked flesh-stitching machine. The alien's head dripped blood
– Callum noticed he'd destroyed one of its eyes. The head hung
lower, but watched him as it approached, clumping past bodies
more warily this time. It learnt quickly. This had to be fast. Only
one more chance. And time was running out in other ways.
The beaks were building another hybrid thing, but maybe they'd
informed the adults he'd encountered down below, which could
be on their way even now. There might be hundreds on this ship.
Maggie had less than a minute left.

Callum's gaudy shirt was torn and the peace flowers bloody.
He pulled it off, held it in his left hand. Blood and sweat coated
his upper body, slick. More seconds gone. The alien was almost
upon him when Callum dashed forward, aware of the creature's
speed and hoping to be just that bit quicker. Its blow missed
and he was within that deadly arm reach, the limbs enclosed
him, whirring, sharp bits cutting in as it gripped, but he ignored
that; wrapped the shirt around its head, tight, twisting it so the
thing couldn't see, and the snapping jaws in front of his face were
muffled. Callum was pushing back, using the light path to give
him momentum, trying to overbalance the creature, forcing it
to take steps back to right itself. It couldn't move back from him
far enough, staggered on bits of body, the stitching mandibles
close, loudly clicking, while the alien tried to reach the rags on its
face but he was already stabbing with the screwdriver, thud thud
punching holes through the bloody cloth into that head, the slit
within it, the other eye, blood so hot it burned as it spilled across
his hand; the alien fell, tried to hold on to Callum, pulling him
through the ribs towards the machinery, but Callum was too
slippy with blood and sweat, leaned back, the alien couldn't hold

on and fell against the creature that was nearly finished; the beaks were stitching, sewing them together in a great clattering, and his attacker couldn't get up; it finally pulled off the rag, its head a ruin. As if realising their mistake the beak machines began to break the two bodies apart again but the awoken alien struggled, pulled, tearing their work, causing them problems as if not fully under control, granted individuality they don't want when all flesh is one pool of blood. It dragged its body tangled and meshed to another, strings pulled from spools in those triangular needles, unable to escape the frenzied stitchers. It was lost in gore and thread.

Callum saw Maggie. Trying to get out of her flesh sack. So near to the machinery. He grabbed her oily arms, no time to cut more, pulled her back while she kicked, creating space, falling and standing, until they were at the side of the last lane and on firm black surface, beetle-like shell; she was in his arms, the veiny slimy cowl dragging behind her; she gasped like her first breath, a memory of pain and triumph and Cerys' euphoric smile in Callum's mind, that smile, that day ... a good day. He kissed Maggie on her forehead, ignoring the goo, loving the sound of her breathing, her sobs, and the feel of his child in his arms. But he had the sinking feeling that had plagued him throughout this long night: there was not enough time. Movement all around. They had to go.

He pulled Maggie up, took her hand, and ran, trying to ignore those unfortunates still trapped. He couldn't rescue others, it took too long to cut through. He had to look ahead, at the girl beside him, not at those he was leaving; not give in to the sickening horror of their fate.

Maggie staggered, her limbs stiff from confinement, and the strangeness of running on these glowing blue force field lanes, but she didn't fall. Callum avoided looking at the many cuts and tears in his chest and arms. Hopefully it appeared worse than it was.

The ship vibrated in a way he hadn't noticed before. A pulsing readiness. He ran faster.

Which way? There might be a way off in any direction. But the ship was so big he could end up lost. No, stick to your trail, and have faith. It took a few moments of panic before he spotted the gap in the cavernous outer wall, identifiable by the light path running away from him. He hoped it was the same one he'd entered by – there seemed to be others, all feeding into this room. Along the corridor, curving to the right this time. Another vibration, which set up a faint thrumming he could feel through the soles of his boots. And he noticed there were no bodies on the light path. Maybe it was a different tunnel after all, or maybe ... there were no more bodies. They were being used up. The stores were full. In which case the creatures might be getting ready to leave.

No time for caution like on his way in. Maggie seemed to have recovered, back to her agile self, and it was Callum who now struggled to sprint next to her. There was no need to talk, he realised; they communicated without words. Understood. That was a closeness he'd yearned after for years, though not under these circumstances.

The portals to their sides remained closed. The light path flickered and went out. It felt like they'd run for miles, and

Callum's chest was beyond pain, struggling to pull in enough hot and stale air to fuel his burning legs for a bit longer.

"You go on," he told Maggie in gasps, but she shook her head, kept hold of his hand, was pulling him now. So sure, her feet pounding on the ship's hard shell, legs striding like one of those professional runners on TV. She had the spurs of youth and panic. Callum could hardly feel either of those any more. The night had been too long.

The corridor's curve lengthened as they moved from the tighter spiral, and he realised they were past the point where he'd first opened his eyes; before them was a hole. About ten feet wide, a hole in the middle of the floor, showing swirling fog. Above it was some kind of machinery, a globe with parts that ran into the ship's surface. Must be something to do with how he'd been pulled up. There were no visible controls. He wished he'd kept his eyes open, learned more.

He knelt, heart hammering, leaned forward. Down to the field far below. But it was moving slowly, and he estimated it was in pace with the vibration running through the ship. A hole, but it didn't act like one, no air or breeze or sound reached him through it. He lay on his stomach, reached down. Where he touched it his skin tingled, but wasn't restricted. His hand passed through whatever invisible barrier was there, and beyond the tingling was coolness, freshness. Looking down there was a moment when the clouds flickered, clear, as if in the backdraught from the craft's passing motion. A glimpse of grass passing below, darkness, the pale matchsticks of a goal post. Too high. A hundred feet up, maybe, and slowly rising as well as moving horizontally. Above the field, heading east. Clouds folded back below, obscuring the view. He tried to imagine where they were, what was next. Sat up, feet dangling over the edge. Maggie sat beside him and held his hand. Movement in the corridor behind. One of the things emerging through a door. He looked back, saw it pounding towards them. Eyes large, jelly-like, white phosphorescence with small dots in the centre; head swollen, fleshy, somehow aquatic; he wondered if it was the one that had been searching along his line, saw that it had a beard-like growth under its chin, made up of cables, or fingers, or tentacles, or all three. It couldn't have been made from anything on Earth, surely? There was no time.

Maggie had her eyes closed, shivered; he knew she was readying herself to die. Geography in his head, a glance down again, something visible for a second, yes.

"Good job it's not your mother I had to rescue," Callum said, gripping Maggie's hand so tight it must be crushing her; then he slipped forward and pulled her after.

She screamed then, eyes open. They fell from the cloud, luckily hadn't risen too far; and he saw the dark line he'd hoped for below, the swollen river Pengymer that fed down from his hills to the town, fat and deep from autumn rains. It seemed to fly towards them, Callum pulled Maggie tight, tried to wrap himself around her, protect her, couldn't breathe as air rushed past. Drown or not; miss the river and break on the ground or not; it was better than what would have happened if they'd stayed. He'd be proud to die with his daughter. He squeezed.

They hit, hard; inhaled water in shock, but he didn't let go; she struggled, but he didn't let go, didn't lose her; touched the bottom, mud and rocks and dark, using it to kick up, to pull her, and he didn't let go; and although it was body panic, the cold seemed to bring him alive, because it *was* cold, stunned away the alien heat, replaced pain with numbness; this was Earth. He didn't let go. Up, along, breaking the surface, pulling Maggie, both choking, though he was laughing too; he half swam, half dragged until they could crawl, get out through the slime. Shivering up to the line of the path that bordered the river, hands sinking into mud and wet leaves, further, until they both collapsed, shivering. But when he looked at her, coughing water from her lungs, she was happy, like him.

And he realised he could see her face, not in blue, but in yellow. They looked up together. The ship was accelerating away, like a part of Earth that just lifted up and flung itself from us, unable to take the centrifugal forces that glue us to this world. Around it the low clouds followed; between those clouds and the ground was a line of crackling electricity, connecting the two, like when two wood blocks sandwiched by glue are pulled apart, stretching but reluctant to let go, holding on until it's too much and the holes outnumber the substance and finally breaks. Yellow lightning blooming from momentary glows above, tongues of electricity tasting our ground. Callum was thankful for a colour other than blue; thankful that it was going. In the distance were small speckles that could be similar lightning patches; then the sky began to clear, the low clouds were dissipating, dissolving into vapour, showing black sky beyond. Not just black though: the pale white of a full moon, and beyond that a sky full of stars, visible for once in the total absence of Earth's artificial lights. A streak in the sky as something left, burning; others on the horizon. Those burning lights faded to stars too. And there was a cool breeze down here at last.

Callum took Maggie's shaking hand. Pointed up at the sky with his other, at the spot that had always stood out for him, intersecting lines that weren't random to the trained eye. "That's Perseus," he told her, before passing out.

CERYS

It was colder now the first light was edging across the clear autumnal sky. Callum and Maggie both shivered uncontrollably. Goosebumps all down Callum's arms, Maggie's legs: there'd be repercussions from this. His throat was already thickening, and Maggie was sniffing continuously.

He squeezed her shoulder harder. It was great. It meant they were still alive.

At first glance it was as if nothing had happened. The houses still stood, lines of grey stone and slate. Cars up on kerbs, roads clear, trees dropping their last yellowing leaves. But then you'd notice the details, which didn't fit your small Welsh town expectations. Broken windows, glass ready to crunch underfoot on narrow pavements. Front doors ajar, only gloom beyond. A darkened patch on the road, which teased out to a smear as if something was dragged.

They limped on.

There were a few people now, leaving homes warily, looking down the road, up at the sky, behind them. Rabbits from burrows. Lucky ones. Few spoke. Just a nod, eyes wide. Shocked. What could you say, anyway? How could anyone whoop for joy when there had been so much loss? If the few people he passed were representative, then nearly everyone had been taken. This was no party. It was a wake.

Past the bike hire shop. Mo's bakery. Traditional stone solidity of the memorial bridge. Then he could see the dark finger pointing upwards: an accusation, a beckoning, who knew? It had been years since he'd come here. The church doors were open. There were pews inside, an unruly pile. Then he saw that one of the heavy doors was splintered off its hinges.

"Michael? Cerys?"

He walked faster. Told Maggie to wait outside. She ignored him.

There were people. A moan. A smell of blood. It wasn't them. It couldn't be them.

Callum gripped someone's shoulder firmly but gently, moved them aside to see who they knelt around in the darkness.

An old woman.

"Michael!" Callum shouted, turning away. "Cerys!" His voice echoed from above.

Outside, he shouted again, louder. Maggie joined him. They walked, took it in turns. Glances from the walking wounded, the silent shocked. And then he saw the pyjamas, recognised their colour first, pattern, size, face and hair after, boy in slippers, face so pale, like a moon, not running like he should have been. Callum went to him. Drew him in. "Son, it's all right. Everything will be all right."

"The vicar prayed to God," Michael whispered. "And nothing happened."

Just as long as your favourite is safe, eh?

Callum looked at his face. Lost. "Where's your mother?" Maggie had joined them, was hugging her brother and saying she was sorry, but Michael just stared at Callum.

"They got in."

"To the church?"

Michael nodded. "The doors. Broke them down. Seemed silly, the windows were the weak point, but they chose the door, and I –"

"Cerys?"

"They got in and there were a few of us. It was – I was with Mum. She was screaming at them. And she pushed me away from her. I tried to hold on, I was so scared, but she pushed me away. And then I understood. She screamed and swore while I crawled behind a bench, and it was *her* they went after when she started running. They moved away from me, towards her and the others. And I just hid, Dad. The things didn't stay long, didn't search. Just grabbed people and left." Michael's eyes had been staring at his memories, but then he focussed on Callum. "Mum did it to save me. But I didn't want to leave her on her own. I would have stayed but I was too scared. How could she do that?"

"She's the bravest woman I've ever known," Callum said, straining to keep his voice steady, keep everything from collapsing. He'd held on for so long. "A good person ... accepts pain in *themselves* before they ... before they accept it in others." It was no good. Callum put his face against his son's neck, smelt the dirt, sweat, and fear, but it was also his flesh, his and Cerys', and it didn't matter if he cried. "We should have loved her more," he mumbled into Michael's shoulder, feeling Maggie's pressure on his back, knew she was crying too. "I should."

THE LONG WAIT

Things had started working again. People had assembled, were going to fortify one of the buildings, arm themselves.

Callum found their bicycles and they headed back to the farm in silence. Cerys' old shopper was left leaning against a lamp post for someone else to use.

Callum heated up some food. It was tasteless. Gathered tools, but just found himself staring up at the sky. Grey, now. All grey with clouds. He shuddered.

"It was like they were collecting us."

Michael, who'd managed to approach Callum without him noticing. That was no good. He needed to be more alert than ever. Being tired was no excuse. Being sad was no excuse. He owed it to her to have strength.

"Don't think about it," Callum said.

"Harvesting us."

His son was too wise for a teenager. Callum owed him the truth. Maybe not the full truth of what he'd seen on the ship, but enough to prepare him. "Yes."

"What will we do? The house is a mess."

Callum had been dismayed at the damage inside. Destruction wrought by anger, frustration. He'd really pissed those things off with their escape from the farm.

"We'll rebuild." Callum mussed his son's hair for a second, then withdrew his hand awkwardly. It felt wrong now. As if he were doing it to an adult. "We'll rebuild everything. And be thankful for the whole lot."

"Will they come back?"

They both looked up at the sky. "I don't think so," Callum told him.

Michael seemed reassured by that. Returned to the house.

Callum knew the sky was big. Went on forever. And they were so small. He had to manage the worry carefully. But this afternoon he would start digging trenches, put out barbed wire, see about fitting bars on the doors and windows. When tonight came he hoped he wouldn't need it. But looking at that expanse of flat greyness, knowing it could hide anything, he didn't feel as certain as he'd sounded when speaking to Michael.

She was on the ship somewhere.

She had been on the ship even as he was escaping with Maggie. Maybe they'd run past her. Maybe she saw them leave her.

He was grinding both hands into fists. Realised there was a screw in one of them, which had pierced his flesh. He dropped the metal, sucked on the neat puncture, tasted the metallic blood.

If they came back, it might be a chance to get Cerys.

He'd crack if he didn't hold on to that hope. Couldn't bear to think of her out there in the constellations, endless alien cold, an absence of heat, air, light, love. Yes, he'd try, if they came back. He just hoped she'd still recognise him.

And that he'd recognise her.

ABOUT THE AUTHOR

Karl Drinkwater is an author with a silly name and a thousand-mile stare. He writes dystopian space opera, dark suspense and diverse social fiction. If you want compelling stories and characters worth caring about, then you're in the right place. Welcome!

Karl lives in Scotland and owns two kilts. He has degrees in librarianship, literature and classics, but also studied astronomy and philosophy. Dolly the cat helps him finish books by sleeping on his lap so he can't leave the desk. When he isn't writing he loves music, nature, games and vegan cake.

Go to karldrinkwater.uk to view all his books grouped by genre.

As well as crafting his own fictional worlds, Karl has supported other writers for years with his creative writing workshops, editorial services, articles on writing and publishing, and mentoring of new authors. He's also judged writing competitions such as the international Bram Stoker Awards, which act as a snapshot of quality contemporary fiction.

Don't Miss Out!

Enter your email at karldrinkwater.substack.com to be notified about his new books. Fans mean a lot to him, and replies to the newsletter go straight to his inbox, where every email is read. There is also an option for paid subscribers to support his work: in exchange you receive additional posts and complimentary books.

OTHER TITLES BY KARL DRINKWATER

STANDALONE SUSPENSE
Turner
They Move Below
Harvest Festival

MANCHESTER SUMMER
Cold Fusion 2000
2000 Tunes

CONTEMPORARY SHORT STORIES
It Will Be Quick

NON-FICTION
From Idea To Item

COLLECTED EDITIONS
Karl Drinkwater's Horror Collection
Lost Solace Five Book Edition

AUTHOR'S NOTES

This story had been fermenting in my head for years after I couldn't sleep one night and played a game of "What if?" What if I heard noises outside: shuffling zombies, coming to eat my brain? What would I do? It led to fantasies of barricading myself in the attic, drinking water from the tank, sneaking out for supplies.

But by the time I came to write it, during NaNoWriMo 2015, I felt that zombies were too well-known; the story had been told before, and was possibly too static if you spent most of your time hiding in one place. I wanted something faster, a different threat. Then I remembered a recurring dream I have about aliens coming to Earth (often beginning with strange cloud patterns) and the words kept coming until this simple story about a man keeping his family together reached the logical conclusion.

Thanks

I am grateful to Rosemary Alldred for bringing the story to life in her wonderful audiobook version. Try it out! Also thanks to you, for reading. Without my fans, I'd just be talking to myself.

www.ingramcontent.com/pod-product-compliance
Lightning Source LLC
Chambersburg PA
CBHW030607130626
46552CB00006B/2687